I was thoroughly frightened now. The woods were dark and seemed to come horribly alive, resenting my intrusion. Birds screeched and the wind flung a handful of dry evergreen needles at my face.

I stumbled to my feet, sobbing. I had to get out of this place—I *had* to! The sounds around me were loud, like someone crashing toward me. I screamed as I thought of the man I was sure had watched me earlier. Was he stalking me, waiting to pounce?

Annie's words whispered in my ears . . . "There's evil at Harrowgate . . . death . . . "

I bolted, fighting my way out of the thicket, stumbling and crawling, pulling myself erect. I could hear the heavy sound of steps snapping dead branches, rustling thick leaves.

I could scarcely breathe, so great was my fright. A huge shadow appeared on the path in front of me, dark and menacing. I screamed and felt terror envelop me as I slid to the ground, collapsing in a faint. . . .

The Mistress of Harrowgate

BY JESSICA LAURIE

ZEBRA BOOKS

KENSINGTON PUBLISHING CORP.

ZEBRA BOOKS

are published by

KENSINGTON PUBLISHING CORP.
475 Park Avenue South
New York, N.Y. 10016

Chapter One

I drew my serge cape about me and huddled in the corner of the train seat. The drafty car swayed and creaked through the night, bringing me closer to Harrowgate.

Harrowgate. How strange to be going back after four years. It seemed a much longer time since I'd left to be on my own, first to school and then taking a job in London with Miss Orney's Academy. I sighed as I thought about these past weeks and the terrible upheaval of my life. I had so wanted to be independent and free of the demands that had hampered me at home, free to make my own decisions and mistakes. Pain gathered under my breast. Could I term my all-too-short romance with Edward Law a mistake? Tears scalded at my eyelids. Yes, Edward had been a mistake. I knew that now, no matter how eager I had been to believe his promises. And I was paying dearly for my mistake by fleeing my position and London to hide once more at Harrowgate.

The letter from Juliette had come at my darkest moment and seemed like an answer to prayer. She begged me to come back—my grandfather was dead. Her note had been a quickly scrawled plea for someone in the family to take over the terrible responsibilities that had fallen on her shoulders.

It was difficult to imagine Harrowgate without my grandfather, Franklin Ashcroft. He had ruled the estate as long as I could recall and had taken me and my brother in to raise when our parents were killed in a riding accident when Charles and I were adolescents. Unaccustomed to youngsters about, he set strict rules of behavior to which we were expected to conform. We were clothed, fed and educated, but we were never really loved. Charles, the elder by two years, had rushed off to join the service as soon as he was of age, leaving me alone in the great house with the old man. When I asked permission to go to school in London, he seemed relieved to be rid of his responsibilities at last. When Charles met and fell in love with Juliette Ilford while he was on leave from the army, no one could have been more surprised than I that he returned to Harrowgate to ask grandfather's permission for his fiancé to stay there until his return from fighting the Boers in South Africa. Now the war was said to be winding down. Charles would be mustered out of the Army in several months, and he and Juliette would wed.

I wondered if he intended to stay on at Harrowgate? He and I were the last of the

Ashcrofts. The estate would go to him, of course, to do with as he pleased. If his memories were as distasteful as mine, he would sell it and never look back.

I stared at the countryside shrouded in gray mist. I did not recognize any landmarks, even though I had made the train trip several times before when I was young. The swirling fog made the darkness ominous, and the old coach creaked alarmingly. For the hundredth time I told myself there was nothing to worry about. The train was perfectly safe, and I would be at my destination soon.

The coach was dimly lit and almost empty. An elderly woman dozed at the far end of the car, her gray head, covered by a black shawl, bobbing gently with the motion. Occasionally the unsmiling conductor made his way through the length of the train, yet I felt completely alone. Isolated, as I had been in London since Edward had found someone to replace me in his heart. How I missed our outings in Hyde's Park and to the Empire Music Hall. I longed for Edward's quick laughter and charming smile. I missed his touch—

I huddled in my cloak in an attempt to ease the chill I felt inside. Beyond the window, the mist turned to rain and began to streak the grimy glass. As I listened, it seemed I could hear it drive relentlessly on the roof of the train coach, but I knew it was only an echo of the clacking wheels. Was the storm a portent of my visit to Harrowgate? I shuddered at the thought.

The car lurched suddenly. Almost at the same instant, the door opened and an icy gust of wind swept through. A tall, handsome, dark-haired man with compelling eyes made his way down the aisle. He wore a long frock coat with a heavy wool scarf about his throat and a rain-spattered beaver hat pulled low on his head. His gaze swept over me as he approached, and I was startled to see his eyes quicken. He stood transfixed, staring at me with a piercing gaze, and I found I could not look away. My pulse raced suddenly, as though he were somehow seeing into my thoughts, and I felt my face flush.

At last he seemed to realize he was staring. He touched the brim of his hat with a brief, courtly bow and his full lips curved in a hesitant smile. "There's no heat in the car ahead," he said softly. "It seems warmer here."

I nodded, unable to think of a sane reply. He moved on slowly and sat several rows behind me.

I looked out the window again and tried to concentrate on the patterns of rain on the glass. My shimmering reflection stared back at me, then went hesitantly to the man's. His face was turned toward me as though he too were watching me. I lowered my gaze quickly. Why in the world would an absolute stranger stare at me so? Did he find me attractive? I blushed again at the notion. His first look had been of surprise and perhaps a tinge of anger. He hadn't expected to see me, that much was certain. Did he know me, or had he mistaken me for someone else? I wanted to turn and look at him again, but I could not bring myself to do it. If his eyes met mine, he would think me exceedingly bold, and I would be dreadfully embarrassed.

It was possible that he was simply a brash man who ogled women at any excuse. I had been termed pretty by others, though I thought my eyes too widely spaced and my mouth too full. Still, I had the delicate features of all the Ashcrofts, the same fine bone structure and the rich, auburn hair of my father and my brother Charles—who was, indeed, a handsome young man. We were often remarked alike enough to be twins, despite the difference in our ages.

I turned to the window again and concentrated my attention on the storm. It had broken with full fury now. Thunder rolled and crashed menacingly. The lashing rain, driven by invisible gusts of wind, bowed the glistening, soaked trees. Their motion seemed to moan and keen with the weather. A jagged, steely flash of lightning gave me a glimpse of the laboring locomotive and the gleaming tracks laid out like an ugly wound across the lowlands. It couldn't be much farther; the ride already seemed twice the distance I remembered.

Another cold draft swept through the car

and the sudden sound of the clacking wheels filled it as the door at the rear of the car opened. The conductor called out, "Louthwick, next stop. Louthwick." He walked past, glancing at me to be sure I'd heard, then left by the door ahead. The heavy door clanked shut behind him.

I sighed inwardly with relief. Louthwick was the tiny village that stood in the valley below Harrowgate. As a child, I had gazed at it from the high arched windows of the manor house. I had never been permitted to go to the village unescorted or make friends among the village children. My grandfather considered them too 'common' for the members of the Harrowgate household.

But grandfather was dead and buried now in the tiny churchyard at the foot of the hill. I would visit his grave and place flowers on it dutifully, paying off the last of my obligation to him. Perhaps the hurts and angers of the past would be buried with him.

Another sigh escaped my lips. I wished Charles were here. He was always so much better at coping than I, especially with the querulous old man who'd given us a home. Charles would know exactly what to do now. I was confused and unsure. I knew only that I could not expect Juliette, who was not yet a member of the family, to handle Harrowgate's problems alone.

I wondered again why Charles had brought her here instead of having her stay in London until his return. It was strange, but no concern of mine if the plan suited the two of them. I had only met Juliette once, very briefly, when Charles brought her to Miss Orney's Academy to tell me that they were going to Harrowgate. She was a shy, pretty girl with dark hair and deep blue eyes that hinted of Irish blood, and a milk-white complexion with a lovely touch of bloom at her cheeks. She had said very little and had eyes only for Charles, to whom she clung tightly as though afraid he might leave her behind. She was excited about the prospect of going to Harrowgate, and I wondered what Charles had told her about it. But I'd been too preoccupied with my own life and Edward to do more than wonder about it.

The train screeched and rocked as it began to slow down. When the lurching and shuddering finally stopped, I rose to reach down the small valise on the rack over my head. From the corner of my eye, I saw the tall man who'd stared at me doing the same, and I was dismayed. He was getting off at Louthwick. Did he live in the village? Had he known or seen me when I lived at Harrowgate? I quickly told myself I was making too much of the notice he'd paid me. He had probably been wool-gathering and not even noticed me until I stared back.

When the train finally braked to a stop, I walked to the door and had no choice but to stand close to the man who followed me down the aisle. I stared straight ahead as the con-

11

ductor placed the step and held out his hand to me. The man came directly behind me and spoke in a soft undertone to the conductor before he strode down the platform. I breathed with relief as he disappeared around the end of the station.

It was icy cold. The wind bit through my cape and spatters of rain whistled under the overhang and stung my face. I glanced around, but there was no carriage waiting nor any familiar face from the manor house. The station was deserted when the train pulled away slowly. I shivered and pushed open the door to the tiny waiting room.

A single lamp was burning low behind the glass-enclosed cage where the station master usually sat, and the shutter was drawn. The room was cold and drafty, and I felt terribly alone as the light from the train windows faded in the distance. I had not thought about a carriage to take me up the hill. I had been foolish to rush off on the first available train without writing first to tell Juliette I was coming. Now I was stranded in the middle of the night. Juliette had sounded so desperate and I had been so anxious to get away, I had not considered the consequences of my hasty action.

Shivering, I drew my cape tight and went out onto the platform again. My trunk had been unloaded and stood against the station wall where the trainmen had pushed it under the shelter of the overhanging roof and out of the dampness. The wind howled mournfully. Nothing moved in any direction but the swaying trees.

Without warning, a figure stepped from the darkness, startling me so I stifled a scream. It was the tall, dark man from the coach. He was hunched in his coat, his hands deep in his pockets and his scarf wound partly across his face to protect him from the wind and rain.

"If you're going to Harrowgate," he said, "you'd best come with me."

Chapter Two

He took the valise from my hand and led the way to a carriage drawn up in the deep shadows behind the station. The horse pawed restlessly and the driver, sitting huddled in his great coat and cap against the wet night air, steadied the animal with the reins.

My companion opened the door and made a hesitant gesture to help me climb up, but I was already pulling myself onto the high step. I had accepted his offer unquestioningly, partly from surprise that he knew my destination without asking. I had little choice since I had no desire to attempt the long walk in the dark, chill night, nor did I fancy sitting in the bleak station until it opened in the morning. Still I did not want to seem the bold type with whom this man could take liberties.

I sat deep in the corner of the seat and pulled my skirt and cape around my legs. With an amused glance, the man sat back and slammed the door. He tapped the roof to signal the driver, and the carriage jerked into motion.

He stared ahead at the small patch of grey

landscape illuminated by the coach lights. I forced myself to speak.

"How did you know I was going to Harrowgate?"

He turned to me with a curious smile. "You're Margaret Ashcroft. I recognized you."

Startled, I asked, "Have we met?"

"When you were a child."

A most unsatisfying answer. I tried again. "Perhaps I'd remember your name. . . ."

His smile widened. "Wiley Temple."

I searched my memory but found nothing to give me any further clue to his identity. "Were you a friend of my grandfather's?"

He seemed to relax just a trifle. "I was his lawyer. I am handling affairs at Harrowgate since his death, at least until you and your brother return." He watched me for a reaction, and when none was forthcoming, he added, "At Juliette's request, of course."

"I see." I still had no recollection of having seen him before or of hearing his name, but there were many things about my grandfather I did not know. I had never been privy to his personal affairs. But if Wiley Temple had recognized me on the train, why hadn't he spoken then? On impulse, I said, "You weren't pleased to see me in the coach. Why?"

He resumed staring out the window and did not answer. I found myself wavering between appreciation and dislike for this strange man. The rain came again in a sudden burst, rattling like hail against the carriage. It seemed to snap him from his reverie.

He turned back to me and asked, "Does anyone know you're coming?"

"Yes, of course."

He frowned and peered at me. "No one met you."

"I—didn't have time to write. Juliette sounded so distraught, I took the first train."

"Ahhh, Juliette sent for you."

"Do I need an invitation to my grandfather's house?" I was piqued at his remarks and his rudeness. He was cross-examining me as if he had some prior right to Harrowgate and I was an intruder.

"No, of course not."

We lapsed into silence as the coach jogged along the rutted road. I could feel the horse straining as the carriage moved uphill, the wheels occasionally slipping in the mud. We would be at Harrowgate soon, just through the wooded area and beyond the sweeping curve of the road. I would be glad to escape the close confines of the carriage and my companion's company.

"You'll find Harrowgate changed," Wiley Temple said after a bit.

I looked at him. "In what way?"

He considered his answer, then said carefully, "It's quite different with your grandfather gone."

It seemed a weak argument, but he didn't choose to elaborate. I had the strange feeling he was trying to frighten me, and I didn't know why.

The carriage lumbered and the wheels creaked. The rain whipped against the windows and roof in a steady drumroll. The wind had risen, and damp gusts whistled through the doors and windows of the coach. I shivered. We seemed destined to ride in gloomy silence unless I pursued the conversation. Curious, I finally asked, "Have you been staying at Harrowgate?" I really wanted to ask *why* he was going to the manor house, but I lacked the courage.

He frowned as though pondering a weighty problem. "I've been there several months."

"Were you here at the time of my grandfather's death?"

"Yes."

I could not resist chiding him. "I should have been informed sooner. Poor Juliette. . . . How dreadful to be forced to cope with so many problems alone." I was thinking of the shy, delicate girl who'd clung to Charles's strength.

Wiley Temple ignored my criticism. He looked at me sharply. "She has not been well."

"Juliette—?" I sat up with a start. "I had no idea. How terrible. How long has she been ill?"

"She nursed your grandfather throughout his illness. He was sick several months before he died. It was a great strain on her."

I felt a rush of impatience. "Why was I not notified?!" If news of Grandfather Franklin's illness had reached me, would I have gone to

17

him? Ashamed of my own doubts, my cheeks flushed.

He shrugged. "The decision was Juliette's."

Almost abruptly, the storm subsided and the sudden silence inside the coach was startling. I glanced out the window and saw that the rain had slackened to a fine mist. The wind still swayed the wet trees, but here and there through dimly seen clouds, I caught the wink of a star. A large rift appeared as I watched, and the cold, distant moon shone through.

Inexplicably, the moon was comforting; I felt my tension ease. Watching the thick trees and brush that hugged the road, I thought of Juliette. I'd see her shortly and I could assess the situation for myself. If she was ill, I'd see she had proper care. I owed her that.

The carriage leaned as the horse negotiated a wide turn that lay a quarter of a mile from the house. I had a momentary view of the road ahead. I blinked. A figure was standing in the middle of the road, its arms upraised as though to halt the carriage or turn it back. It was the figure of a man, with wispy white hair and a long white beard blown about his face by the wind. He was wearing a long white robe of some sort.

I bolted up as the horse plunged ahead. "Stop! Stop the carriage!" I cried.

Startled, Wiley Temple rapped for the driver quickly. The carriage groaned to a halt. Temple looked at me. "What is it?"

"A man—there in the road—" I was straining to see the old man's face, but his features seemed part of the mist that swirled around him.

Wiley drew back the curtain and peered out. Scowling, he said, "Where? What man?"

The driver grunted impatiently and the horse stirred.

"There—" I pointed ahead where the road curved past a copse of birch. The figure had not moved, except for the waving arms that motioned us back.

Wiley looked out the window again, then shook his head. "I fear you're overtired from your long journey. There's no one there." He sat back and tapped the box. "Go on, driver!" The carriage lurched directly toward the white figure.

"NO!" I screamed and pressed my hand to my mouth as the figure vanished suddenly, leaving only curling tendrils of mist across the road.

Wiley was watching me closely. I shivered. Without taking his eyes from me, he said, "It was your imagination. I saw nothing."

I shook my head. "I don't imagine things. I never have before." I could not make up my mind if he was laughing at me.

He continued to stare. "The journey from London is tedious and you are under a great strain, learning of your grandfather's death like this. Fatigue plays tricks on the mind."

I turned away. I did not want to believe the

possibility of truth in what he said. I *had* seen the figure—I still saw him in my mind's eye: thin and fragile, his face twisted in fear. No, that was impossible, I realized. I hadn't seen his features at all. Yet I was sure I recognized the attitude of fear.

Was it my own fear mirrored in my thoughts? Had I imagined the figure warning me away from Harrowgate because I did not want to return and was only doing so out of a sense of duty?

I closed my eyes and bit my lip. Wiley must think me a fool! Well, let him. I didn't care what he thought. I heard him say, "ahh—" and opened my eyes. The house was silhouetted angularly against the dark hill. Shadowy oaks vaulted overhead as the carriage turned through the stone gates and started up the curving drive, which was wet with rain and shining in the frosty moonlight.

Lights in the lower floor were dim and mealy like the eyes of a cat, winking as tree branches whipped in the wind. The driver halted the carriage under the wide portico. Wiley opened the door to admit a chilling blast of air. He stepped down and offered his hand to help me out. Then he turned to the driver and handed up some folded pound notes.

I stared at the house. In the darkness, it loomed ominously, the tall turrets black against the cold, moonlit sky. The lanterns beside the front door had not been lit even though Wiley Temple was apparently expected. I suppressed a shudder and tried to dispel my growing sense of dread as I climbed the wide stone steps. The wind whipped at my skirts and numbed my fingers.

Wiley lifted the heavy latch and the door swung inward, unlocked. He seemed very much at home. Unaccountably, I resented it but I could not resist the welcome flood of warm dry air that engulfed me. I stepped inside with relief.

A single lamp in a sconce on the wall cast a pool of yellow light across the dark hall. Still, the house had an empty feeling and an eeriness that disturbed me.

"Is anyone at home?" I asked Wiley.

"I told you it was much changed," he said, doffing his hat and scarf, then hanging the greatcoat on the rack near the door. "Much of the house is unused. I'm afraid the rest hasn't been maintained properly. If you go to the village, you'll hear stories."

"What kind of stories?" I queried.

He smiled laconically. "They say it's haunted."

A shiver ran along my spine. The townspeople had always said such things of Harrowgate, but I had paid little heed. Was Wiley Temple referring to those old tales? Somehow I had the dreadful feeling he was not, but I could not bring myself to ask.

Footsteps came along the uncarpeted hall. Wiley looked around and said, "Ah, good evening, Lionel. I've brought you a guest."

I recognized Lionel Mundy instantly. He'd come to Harrowgate ten years before to work as manservant to my grandfather. His wife, Emma, acted as housekeeper when old Annie became too infirm to handle the work of the big house alone. The Mundys had done their work well enough but had always seemed to have an air of being put upon. I hadn't liked them, nor had Charles. He called them the Moody Mundys when they could not hear him. But the man who stood before me seemed different from the servant I had known. Instead of the withdrawn, quiet man I remembered, his gaze on me was intent and demanding. His piercing eyes seemed to stare through me, and his rough features might have been carved of marble. His face was pale under the dark hair that swept back from his forehead and fell over his coat collar at the neck. There was something almost sinister in his appearance.

"You should have told me you were bringing someone," he said churlishly.

Wiley looked annoyed. "I'm sure you remember Margaret Ashcroft," he said.

Was it my imagination or did Lionel's expression alter? His eyes hardened as he stared at me, frowning, then forcing a smile to his lips.

"I had no idea you were coming. You should have let us know, we would have met you." He glanced at Wiley. "How fortunate that Wiley was on hand—or did the two of you travel from London?"

"We met on the train," Wiley said. "I recognized her immediately."

"Unmistakable. . . ." Mundy said, still staring at me. "It's very good to see you again, Margaret. Welcome to Harrowgate."

How easily he used my name—no longer 'Miss Margaret' as he had once called me. It was as if he no longer considered himself a servant.

"How long has it been?" He pondered the question. "More than four years . . . a long time. I trust you have done well."

I did not care to discuss my private affairs, so I said nothing. He went on as though he had not expected an answer. "I'm sure you must be cold and weary after the long journey." He glanced down the hall. "Emma!"

Emma Mundy appeared from the passageway to the kitchen. She had not changed. Short and plump, her dull hair caught in a tight bun at her neck, she was unsmiling. Her sallow face was plain, and her grey eyes were set deep in her puffy cheeks.

"Miss Margaret has come to visit," Lionel said flatly. "We must make her feel at home."

Emma could not hide her surprise as she bobbed her head in greeting. "It's good to see you again," she said. She picked up my hand satchel from where Wiley had deposited it when we came in. I remembered my trunk on the depot platform and mentioned it.

Wiley said, "I arranged with the coachman to have it brought up in the morning."

"Thank you," I said. "Now, I would like to greet Juliette."

"She's sleeping," Emma said quickly.

"Wiley tells me she's been ill," I said with concern.

At my words, Lionel said, "She's feeling somewhat better these past few days. Nothing to worry about, I'm sure."

"Has the doctor seen her?" There was a doctor in the village, I knew. My grandfather had allowed him to be called when Charles fell from a tree and we feared his leg was broken.

Emma answered. "She won't hear of it. She's positively insistent. But we've told her we'll call him if she doesn't show marked improvement soon."

Lionel looked at me with those piercing eyes again. "Now that you're here, I'm certain it will be a tonic for her to have another young person about. No doubt you'll relieve her of the need to make decisions. It seems to tax her considerably."

Emma lighted another lamp and started toward the wide marble steps that led upstairs. She glanced back for me to follow her. As I went up, I felt the eyes of the two men on my back until I was out of sight.

Why was I so uncomfortable and reading meaning into every glance and spoken word?

Perhaps the incident on the road had un-nerved me more than I cared to admit.

Emma Mundy took me to a room at the front of the house. It was not the room I had occupied when I lived here but one that had been reserved for guests who rarely came. My own room had been small and more cozy after I'd put up bright curtains and added personal touches—pillows, ornaments, sketches. This room was spare and cold, austere with heavy plum colored drapes and bedcovering, and near the bed, a deep-toned rug covering the bare wood floor. Emma set my satchel on a small rack and the lamp on the table. Then she crossed to the fireplace and bent to touch a match to the fire that was already laid in the hearth. The kindling caught immediately and flames crackled over the dry logs, sending off a welcome burst of warmth and light.

"If you are hungry, I can bring you a tray," Emma said.

"Thank you, I'd like that." I gave her a hesitant smile.

It did not elicit one from her. She nodded curtly and went out without further comment.

I stood in front of the fire to drive the chill from my bones, not wanting to remove my cape until the room had warmed. By the dull glow of the lamp, the room was uninviting and cheerless. Perhaps tomorrow I would ask to be moved into my old room. This one would get little sunshine, since it faced the drive and the stately oaks that screened the side of the house. North exposure was dreary at best, even though it afforded a pleasant view of the hill and the village in the distance.

When the frostiness began to vanish from the room, I walked around, touching pieces of furniture, glancing briefly at the faded pictures on the walls. Then I stood at the window where I drew back the drapes so I could look out at the dark night.

The rain had stopped but heavy clouds still scudded across the sky, blanking the moon now and then. The trees and grass glistened wetly and looked dark and cold. It was hard to believe it was spring as I listened to the soft moaning wind in the leaves.

Unexpectedly, I saw a light and I pressed to the glass as I studied the tiny flicker of yellow across the yard. I tried to visualize the arrangement of the house. From this window, my view would include the old east wing that had stood empty and unused as long as I could remember. It was the wing of the house that helped perpetuate the stories the villagers told of the manor house being haunted.

I stared through the wet glass as I tried to determine if the faint, flickering spot was real or a product of my imagination. And if it was real, was it coming from the old east wing? As I watched, it vanished suddenly, and I could not be sure. I let the drape fall in place. I was tired and on edge. This was no time to let my thoughts linger on old legends and ghost stories. I pulled off my cape and hung it on a clothes rack beside the door. I had just changed my damp skirt for a dressing gown of soft green wool and pulled an armchair close to the fire when a tap came at the door.

"Yes?"

Emma Mundy entered with a tray. She set it on the low table before me and would have left without a word had I not stopped her.

"Which room is Juliette using, Mrs. Mundy? I'd like to look in on her before I retire."

She scowled. Her tiny eyes were almost lost in her fleshy face as she frowned. "I don't think she should be disturbed. She needs her sleep."

"I shan't disturb her, I promise."

For a moment I thought she did not intend to answer, but she finally said reluctantly, "The corner bedroom at the rear. The one with the yellow curtains."

My old room. If Juliette was ill, she had more need of its cheerfulness than I. I said nothing about moving from where I was. "Thank you, Mrs. Mundy."

"Will you be down again tonight?"

I shook my head. "No. I am tired and the warm meal will make me drowsy, I'm sure."

She left, and I turned to the light meal she'd brought. Hot soup, cinnamon toast and a mug of hot chocolate—the aromas made my mouth water and I realized how hungry I was. I sat in front of the cheery fire and ate ravenously. When I finished, I longed to crawl into bed

27

and sleep quickly, but I picked up the lamp and made my way down the corridor to Juliette's room. The house was silent. I wondered if everyone had retired, though it was still early by most standards.

At the room I knew so well, I put my hand to the knob and tried to turn it, but nothing happened. The knob was rigid under my touch. The door was securely locked.

Odd. . . . Was Mrs. Mundy sitting with Juliette in order to prevent my seeing her? Nonsense. But the only alternative was just as ridiculous. Why would Juliette bolt herself in for the night?

Puzzled, I retraced my steps. I would not disturb poor Juliette. I would see her in the morning. As I neared the top of the stairs, a cold draught of air swirled upward and the lamp I was holding sputtered and went out suddenly. For a moment, panic assailed me as I stood in the darkness and tried to get my bearings. Downstairs the hall was pitch black, yet I was sure a door had opened and closed, sending up the draught that had extinguished the lamp.

When my eyes grew accustomed to the gloom, I felt my way along the balustrade to the far end of the hall. My outstretched hand searched for the door to my room and I stepped quickly inside. I leaned against the door and slid the bolt securely in place.

I was trembling as I slid under the covers. I did not like being back at Harrowgate with its dark memories and dreary present. Had I anyplace else to go, I would leave as soon as I assured myself that Juliette was all right, but there was nowhere. Like it or not, I had to stay at Harrowgate for now. It was a long time before I fell asleep.

Chapter Three

Something woke me with a start and I bolted up, not knowing what it was but suddenly cold and shivering. I tried to convince myself it had been a dream that was already evading recall, but there had been a sound, I was sure of it.

I looked around the room, peering at shadows and trying to make out the bulky outlines of the unfamiliar furniture. At the drawn curtains, slivers of cold moonlight pierced the darkness. I strained as I listened, but all I heard was the pounding of my heart. An icy trembling beset me once more. I lay back and pulled the covers over me like a frightened child. The room was strange, that was all. The strain of the journey and my own misery were compounded by Wiley Temple's peculiar behavior and the Mundys' arrogant attitudes. It was only natural that I would dream. . . .

Still, I was sure the noise had been real. I huddled in the darkness listening. I knew I would not sleep again until I satisfied myself it was something easily explainable. Finally I slipped out of bed to grope for my robe and slippers and pull them on quickly. The room was cold. The fire had died to ashes. I went to the window and drew back the curtain to let moonlight splash across the dark room. I stared down at the drive and the dark shadows that moved across it. Not the wind in the trees . . . the shadows took definite shape . . . figures. I made out the forms of two men who stood a few yards from the door where the portico did not hide them. They stood close together and their heads were bent as though they were whispering. The sound I had heard was gravel crunching underfoot. As I watched, the two moved along the edge of the drive, their arms gesturing as though they were arguing. I did not have to hear their voices to know they were having an angry confrontation.

They parted quite abruptly. One man moved back toward the house and glanced upward. I stepped back quickly, even though I was sure he could not see me. A moment later I heard the front door open and close softly. The other man hesitated, then continued across the lawn toward the dark, hulking shadows of the old east wing.

I found myself staring into the darkness in which nothing moved. Who were they? I hadn't been able to recognize either of them, but one had come into the house. Wiley Temple or Lionel Mundy? And the other? Why had they found it necessary to meet in the shadows of the drive at this hour? It had to be well past midnight, too late for callers. . . .

As I started back toward the bed, my gaze was drawn inexplicably to a portrait on the opposite wall. Some trick of the moonlight made the face glow as if someone stood there gazing back at me. I moved closer, impelled by I knew not what. Startled, I thought for a moment that I had mistaken a mirror for a picture. The face that looked back at me was my own!

My breath caught as a small gasp escaped my lips. It was not a mirror—the girl in the picture was me! I moved closer and stared in fascination at the sad young face with the unmistakable Ashcroft features that everyone always saw in me. The girl looked about my age. She was wearing a fancy ballgown of elaborate silk and lace, a pearly cream color that enhanced her fair skin and auburn hair. The dress had green ribbons at the neckline and waist, and a lacy green shawl covered her bare shoulders.

She'd sat for the portrait with her hands folded lightly in her lap, her eyes staring directly out so they seemed to capture mine. At the neckline of the gown, a glittering diamond pendant hung against her pale flesh. It dazzled with light the artist had captured within the stone. On one hand, a ring with a stone almost as large glittered. I sensed an incredible sadness in her expression, and I wondered what had caused such sorrow to fill her.

I tried to recall if I had seen the portrait earlier. I had done little more than glance at the pictures, and with only a single lamp and the firelight, this end of the room had been in gloom. I was sure I hadn't noticed the painting of the girl. Nor could I recall ever seeing it before. I realized it might have been moved here after I departed from Harrowgate. The attic was crammed with dusty mementos of the manor house's past.

I could not dispel the odd feeling that the girl was staring at me and forcing me to share her sorrow . . . trying to tell me something.

I laughed at my foolishness. It was only a portrait. I turned away but found myself glancing back in spite of myself. No matter where I went in the room, her compelling gaze seemed to follow me. I returned to the bed and began to climb in, but found I could not. Impelled by a curiosity I could not explain, I walked to the door and slid back the bolt. Moving into the hall, I went to the balcony that overlooked the foyer. It was empty, the door closed and the silence heavy. Moonlight seeped through the thick, mullioned windows and lay like a patterned carpet on the stone floor. Nothing stirred in the silence.

I shivered and hugged my arms across my breasts. There was nothing amiss, no cause for uneasiness. Whoever had come in from the drive was abed by now, and his errand undoubtedly had a reasonable explanation. My curiosity and imagination were running away with me. I turned back to my room, then halted abruptly, frozen in terror. At the end of the gloomy hall, a figure moved toward me with a steady, soundless gait. I stifled a scream. Icicles stabbed along my spine and my head whirled. My breath rasped in my throat. The man was a stranger, middle-aged and dressed in tight breeches and a brocaded waistcoat under a short, dark jacket. A gold watchchain across the vest swayed as he moved. In his hand he carried a gleaming dagger!

I bolted for my room on trembling legs, flinging the door shut behind me and throwing myself on the bed, trying to scramble under the covers, yet unable to keep myself from looking back. The figure appeared in the doorway and moved inside the room as though the door were wide open. He came to the foot of the bed and stared at me. I saw the dark stains on the knife blade.

Dizzying waves of panic filled me and rose to choke off the screams in my throat. I covered my face with my hands and felt myself falling into blackness.

When I came awake again, panic still beat inside my chest like a wild bird and my heart was hammering. Terrified, I looked quickly around the room but the figure was gone. I was alone. The man had not killed me . . . I had fainted from fright. Everything in the room was bathed in deep shadows. I could no longer see the face of the girl in the portrait clearly, nor did I want to. Somehow my mind connected her with the ghostly figure I had seen in the hall. I was not sure why. Perhaps the costumes . . . both were of a bygone period. Was there a connection between the two?

I forced myself to breathe deeply until my panic subsided. Had the figure been a product of my frightened imagination? It had been so real—yet not real at all. I tried to recall the man's features and found I could not.

At long last I took off my robe and slid under the covers. I pulled them tight about my neck and buried my face in the pillow. I was completely drained . . . exhausted. . . . Despite my lingering terror, I felt myself drifting into sleep. I was dimly aware that I had heard no sound as the figure came along the hall or into the room. He had come through the door without opening it. The man had not been flesh and blood—

Chapter Four

When I woke, daylight filled the room. I had not drawn the drapes again, and I could see the sun splashing the trees beyond the window. I'd slept soundly, my exhaustion blotting out all the disturbing thoughts from my mind and letting me sink into oblivion. The events of the mid-night seemed hazy and dreamlike.

I rose and went to the portrait that had startled me so. Strange . . . the girl in the picture was smiling, yet last night she had seemed so incredibly sad. Had it been a trick of the moonlight and my tired brain? Seen in the light, the girl was smiling and happy. The resemblance to me was still there, though not as marked as I'd believed on my first impression. She was definitely an Ashcroft. I wondered who she was.

And who was the man I'd seen in the hall? The strange figure that moved through closed doors and walked without sound? A ghost? Surely it was the only explanation, but I could not embrace it. I had never seen a ghost before, despite the tales I'd listened to as a child.

I sighed and turned to the washstand. Everything was so strange since my arrival at Harrowgate. Was it possible the strain was more telling than I cared to admit? I could find no reasonable explanation for the wraith-like figure on the road nor the one in the hall. Was there one? And how could I be so mistaken about the face of a painting?

Finally I decided that Wiley Temple's talk of Harrowgate being thought haunted had put thoughts in my head that came to life in my half-wakefulness. Well, I was fully awake now, and that was the end of them. I hung up the towel and turned to the wardrobe.

Two of the dresses I'd put away last night were half off their hangers; another was crumpled in a heap on the floor of the closet. Annoyed, I bent to retrieve it. How could I have been so careless? As I picked up the dress, I saw a crushed shawl on the floor of the armoire. I lifted it and looked at it. It was not mine, I had never seen it before. No . . . I had seen it somewhere. . . . I fingered the lacy green cloth, feeling its softness. As I turned, the portrait across the room caught my gaze. I carried the shawl to it and held it close to the painting. The green shawl was the one in the picture!

I stared as confused thoughts jumbled in my mind. The shawl had not been in the closet last night when I unpacked, I was sure of it. How then had it gotten there? I had not been out of the room except for the few moments it had taken me to walk to Juliette's room and the seconds I had stood gazing down into the foyer in the dark.

Yet the shawl had appeared. . . .

I folded the wispy cloth and put it on a shelf. As I dressed, I deliberately kept my glance from the wardrobe. There were so many things I could not explain it confused me. When I had fastened the hooks at the bodice of the blue shirtwaist, I went to the window and looked out. It was full day, with the sun bright in an almost cloudless sky. The valley below Harrowgate shimmered in the brightness as though the storm had never been. The room was still cold and damp with no morning sun to warm it, and I raised the sash to let in the warmth of the day. I inhaled the crisp, clean air.

I judged it to be past eight but there were no sounds of activity downstairs as I went into the hall. On impulse, I turned to Juliette's door instead of descending. The knob turned readily at my touch.

She was lying in the big bed, her eyes closed and her dark lashes brushing her pale cheeks. She *had* been ill! She was thin and there were deep circles under her eyes and a tight, drawn look on her face even in sleep. One hand lay atop the coverlet, and her fingers were like talons clutching it. The milky complexion was chalky and the bloom had vanished from her cheeks.

I started to leave so I would not disturb her,

but she seemed to sense my presence and her lashes fluttered. Her eyes opened and she glanced at me with a frightened look.

I smiled quickly and crossed to the bed. "Juliette, I got your letter. I've come."

Her face twisted as she strained to recognize me. "Margaret? Is it really you at last?" She raised her head from the pillow but fell back quickly. I rushed to her and patted her hand.

"Yes, I am here. You should have told me sooner that you were ill and that grand-father—"

Pain shadowed her face, and I changed the subject quickly. She was in no condition to be chided about anything. "I'm here now," I said cheerfully. "And we must see about getting you well. I shall see the doctor and have him prescribe a tonic that will put you back on your feet in no time."

She shook her head feebly. "No, I do not want the doctor."

"But you must—"

"Annie—Annie can help—" She clutched at my fingers as though compelling me to agree.

I tried to soothe her. "Yes, all right. I'll get Annie." Annie Newgate had been a servant for the Ashcroft family since my grandfather was a young man. Although she worked in the kitchen, her healing powers were legendary throughout the village, and she was called upon to prepare potions for many ills. My grandfather relied on her completely and turned to the doctor only when Annie's gnarled fingers grew too weak to set broken bones. Shortly before I'd left Harrowgate, Annie had been pensioned off to a cottage across the woods to live out her days in peace.

But if Juliette wanted her, I would see if the old woman was able to come. If not, she might have an elixir that would help Juliette regain her strength.

Juliette was relieved by my promise and tried to smile.

"We'll have you fit in no time," I said with false heartiness. "Charles would be very annoyed with me to find I'd let you come to this state."

At Charles's name, tears welled in her eyes. She trapped her lips between her teeth and tried to disguise the small sob that escaped. "Charles. . . ."

"There now, you mustn't cry. You will be well soon and—"

"I have not heard from him, no letter at all since he left. I am sick with worry."

I was astonished at my brother's lack of compassion. He must know she would worry. "The mails are slow," I said. "Perhaps he's already on his way home. The journey can be delayed by all sorts of things . . . inclement weather—"

She sighed and closed her eyes for a moment. When she opened them, she said softly, "Yes, I've told myself that, but I'm so afraid and confused—" She blinked away the tears and turned to pick up a small glass from the table beside the bed. She turned it over, then held it up as she watched bits of white drift down over the miniature village inside the dome. A snow dome! I hadn't seen one for years! Charles had discovered one in the attic and claimed it as one of his treasures.

Juliette smiled. "Charles gave it to me just before he left," she said softly.

She glanced beyond me to the sunlight streaming in the window. The room was bright and cheerful, the yellow counterpane and curtains the same as when I had lived here. They had a fresh, crisp look, and I knew that Juliette had laundered them and kept the room cheerful, at least until she became ill. Was her depression part of her illness, an aftermath of the months she'd had to nurse a sick old man whose temper had undoubtedly not improved with his ill health?

Her gaze came back to me and she smiled weakly as she grasped my hand. "I'm so glad you've come, Margaret. I will get well now, won't I?"

"Of course you will, such a foolish thing to ask." But her eyes were frightened. She didn't think it foolish at all. My coming meant a great deal to her, more than I imagined it could. I patted her hand again and said, "I will go to Annie immediately. She'll have you up and about in no time. Now tell me, have you had your breakfast?" When she shook her head I asked if she'd like me to have two trays brought up so we could chat while we ate.

41

For a moment I thought she was going to accept eagerly, but the light faded from her eyes suddenly. "I'm so tired . . . another time. . . ."

"Of course." I had unthinkingly taxed her strength. She'd been ill a long time and I could not expect so much of her. "I'll stop in later. Rest now."

"You will get Annie?" It was a plea.

"Yes, this very day."

She lay back smiling.

A soft tap sounded at the door and it pushed open. A round-faced girl in a blue gingham dress and a white apron entered, balancing a tray on one arm. She caught her breath and stifled a cry as she saw me.

" 'Scuse me, Miss. Gave me quite a turn seeing you—" She blushed.

"I'm Margaret Ashcroft," I said.

Her head bobbed. "Miz Mundy told me you'd come." Her dark eyes rolled and she shivered. "In that dreadful storm, oh my—" She turned to set the tray beside the bed, then fussed with the pillows and raised Juliette so she was half sitting, crooning over her as though she were a child. "Now there, you must eat and get back your strength. . . ."

"Yes, Becky," Juliette said docilely.

Becky glanced at me. "Miz Mundy says your breakfast is ready whenever you are, Miss."

"Thank you." I took my leave as the girl again turned to Juliette and began to coax her to eat.

I found the others in the dining room. The long table was set with dishes I remembered as those designated for everyday use, and the heavy silver was badly in need of polishing. Lionel Mundy sat at the head of the table in my grandfather's place, his wife at his right. I was so astonished, I was speechless. The Mundys had never dined with the family. But I was forgetting that so much had changed. Grandfather was dead and Charles was thousands of miles away in a distant land. I supposed it was senseless to stand on ceremony and adhere to customs long abandoned. The Mundys were, after all, running the house. I would not disrupt their patterns.

Wiley Temple seemed to sense my momentary discomfort. He rose and pulled out a chair with a cheerful smile. It lighted his handsome face and made his eyes look like deep pools catching a shaft of sunlight. My gloom was dispelled. I smiled back, hesitantly at first, then warmly. Emma Mundy served me a plate of scrambled eggs and sausage from the sideboard, then resumed her seat.

"Did you sleep well?" Lionel inquired.

"Well—" I began. Emma turned to stare at me and I felt my face flush. "Yes, except for—"

"Except for what?" she demanded quickly. All eyes were on me. Only Wiley's had any warmth.

"I was restless. Normally voices outside would not disturb me—"

"Voices? You must have been dreaming," Lionel said curtly.

I blinked at his uncalled-for rudeness. "But there were," I said more sharply than I intended. "I heard them, and when I looked out the window there were two people. I wondered who was about at that late hour."

Emma stared at her eggs and toast. Her fork made a small scraping sound against the china. Lionel muttered and shook his head. Wiley's expression altered, though the smile stayed on his lips.

"I did see them," I said defensively.

A cynical smile twisted Lionel's face. "You saw something on the road last night, too."

So Wiley had told them of the incident. My temper flared momentarily, but not at him— at Lionel. He was saying it was my imagination. Did Wiley believe that too? Did I? I *had* doubted my own senses last night when I saw the ghostly figure with the knife. Somehow I could not tell them about that and expose myself to their ridicule.

Emma looked up. "You always were an imaginative child, Margaret."

"I know what I saw!" I started, then let the matter drop. How could I argue against them? Determinedly, I changed the topic of conversation. "I stopped in to see Juliette this morning. I'm appalled at her condition. She wants old Annie Newgate to tend her. I promised to fetch her myself, if she will come."

All three faces turned to me in surprise. The

Mundys were obviously displeased, but I could not read Wiley's expression.

"Annie is too old and feeble to nurse anymore," Lionel said angrily. "Besides, she holds a grudge against Harrowgate and has sworn never to set foot here again."

Astonished, I said, "Annie?! Why she spent her life here—why would she say such a thing?" I stared at Lionel and tried to fathom his guarded expression.

Lionel shrugged. "She's a very old woman, she must be close to a hundred. Her mind wanders and she lives in a dream world most of the time. No telling what goes on in her head."

"Surely she came when my grandfather was ill?"

He nodded. "She tended him right up to the end, even though she could barely walk. She wouldn't let anyone in the room but Juliette. The two of them did everything for the old man."

"Then surely she will come now that Juliette needs her. I will go to her myself. Does she still live in the cottage across the woods?"

Grudgingly, Lionel admitted that she did, then returned his attention to his food. Emma poured coffee and passed the cups. Wiley smiled reassuringly and his gaze held mine for a moment.

"I'm sure Annie will do what she can," he said warmly. "How can she refuse the request of one she holds in such high regard. She has always spoken of you with fondness—and of Charles. I suspect the years you lived at Harrowgate were the most important of her life."

His remarks surprised me, since I had never felt particularly close to old Annie, who was devoted to my grandfather. But I knew that Wiley was deliberately trying to ease the tension Lionel had created, and I was grateful.

Immediately after breakfast, I returned to my room to change from my soft kid slippers into sturdy walking shoes. The path through the woods, as I remembered it, was rough, and it would be wet from the recent storm. The maid, Becky, was making up the bed and smiled shyly as I entered.

"I can come back, Miss Margaret—"

"No, please go on with your work. I'll only be a minute." I went to the wardrobe and got my shoes, then sat in the small armchair to put them on. The girl glanced at me from time to time. Once I caught her lingering gaze on the portrait across the room.

"Becky, who is the girl in the portrait?" I asked.

"She might be your sister, it's that much alike you look."

"Has the picture always hung there?"

"Long as I can remember," she said. "Cook says Harrowgate would stand with a good cleaning. Get rid of the past, in a manner of speaking."

I frowned. "You mean pictures like this one?"

She nodded, glancing at the door as though making sure no one might overhear. Then she dipped her head toward the picture. "So young to die that way. . . ."

"You know who she is then?" I was curious.

"Oh yes, Miss. That's Elizabeth Ashcroft, your great aunt. Died tragically only two weeks after her wedding. Died right here at Harrowgate." Her eyes were wide and solemn.

"Here? You mean in this room?" My flesh crawled at the thought as I stared at the serene face of the portrait.

"Oh no, Miss. She died in the woods. Running away, she was. They say it was because of those lovely jewels she's wearing. Her own husband stole them to sell for money, he did."

I vaguely recalled some story that had been whispered by the servants when I was a child. Grandfather always forbade mention of it in his presence, as though it were some black secret that had to be forgotten. I had discounted it as the gossip of servants, but now I wanted to know more.

I placed my foot upon the stool while I tied the lace. "Please tell me the story, Becky. Since I look so much like Elizabeth, I'd like to know her better."

She fairly beamed. She was eager to have her say. "Well, Miss Elizabeth married a handsome young man from London. His name was Harland Beaumont, and she met him at a fancy ball. He fairly swept her off her feet, all romantic like. And when he asked her to marry him, she just said yes. Her father was furious. Damon Ashcroft didn't think Beaumont was good enough for his lovely daughter. But Elizabeth carried on as if she'd die of a broken heart until he gave in. The young couple was married in the big ballroom in the east wing. And such a wedding it was. The villagers tell the story like it was yesterday instead of so many years ago, and some of them not even born." Her eyes rolled as though she was recalling the experience firsthand herself. "The gifts they got from all over the country." She glanced at the portrait. "Her father had that lovely diamond pendant and ring made for her. 'Tis said they were worth a king's ransom."

Becky's face sobered. "Not two weeks later the young couple had a terrible row over the jewels, 'tis said. Elizabeth ran out into the woods. She was never seen alive again."

"What happened?"

The girl shuddered. "Lost her way in the dark. Her father found her the next morning caught in the marsh where she'd fallen and drowned." Becky wrung her hands as though witnessing the terrible scene. "He came back to the house in a rage and blamed Harland Beaumont." Her voice fell to a macabre whisper. "Damon killed Beaumont—stabbed him with a dagger."

48

In spite of myself, I shuddered. "How terrible—"

"Out of his mind with grief, he was. And the jewels were never found." She shook her head gravely. "They were nowhere in the house, even though it seemed there was no way the young husband could have gotten them out. Old Damon swore the jewels were cursed and he rued the day he'd bought them. He claimed if he hadn't, his daughter would still be alive. He closed up the east wing and said it would never again ring with music and laughter now that his beloved Elizabeth was gone. She was his only child, so when Damon died, Harrowgate passed to his brother—your own grandfather's pa. 'Tis said he reopened the east wing, but Damon's curse was on it. At the very first ball, there was a terrible accident. One of the women from the village who'd been invited was killed when a candelabra tipped and set fire to her beautiful gown." Becky shook her head and shivered again as though someone had walked over her grave. "They closed the wing again and left it to the ghosts."

I suppressed another shiver. Looking at the portrait, I was struck by the hint of sadness that was present in Elizabeth's eyes, despite the smile on her lips. It was as if she were hiding some inner sorrow.

"And the ghost of her young man wanders about the halls of the east wing searching for his bride—or some say for the jewels," Becky said solemnly.

"Nonsense, that's superstition."

Her eyes went wide. "He's been seen, Miss. People from the village won't come to Harrowgate once dusk falls, not with Damon Ashcroft's curse keeping the dead from their rest."

With a touch of impatience, I said, "I thought he believed the jewels were cursed when he bought them?" The girl was confusing her stories and her superstitions.

She nodded. "Yes, but he cursed them again. He said no person who touched them would ever find peace until the price of his daughter's blood had been paid. The jewels would bring misery and death to any who owned them, and their ghosts would be damned to wander forever."

She was so serious, I could not laugh at her melodramatic foolishness. Curses and ghosts—indeed! I was convinced now that my own mysterious vision had been caused by weariness; much as I hated to admit it, Wiley and the Mundys were right.

I finished tying my shoes and stood up, drawing a cloak from the wardrobe. My eye fell on the green shawl, and I lifted it out. "Becky, does this belong to someone in the house? I found it among my things this morning."

Becky shook her head. "No, Miss, I've never seen it before."

She did not make any connection with the girl in the portrait, and I did not mention it. I replaced the shawl on the shelf and turned to go. Becky had finished the bed and was fussing about, dusting the tabletops and windowsills.

"If you go into Juliette's room, please tell her that I have gone for Annie."

She looked at me strangely. "Annie lives beyond the woods. . . ."

"I know. It's a lovely morning and I feel in need of exercise."

"You'd best take the carriage and go around by the road, Miss Margaret," she said guardedly.

"I prefer to walk."

She said no more, but she looked thoroughly frightened. I knew she was thinking about the story she'd just told me of Elizabeth's tragic death there. But I was not an hysterical, frightened bride fleeing a quarrel, nor did I hold with superstitions.

Chapter Five

The day was growing warmer although there was still a chill in the air. It was spring, but the leaves were new and pale against the blue sky. A few high clouds scudded in the breeze, white puffs caught in the brilliance of the sun. Harrowgate could be beautiful, with the rolling hills and dark patches of woods. I crossed the wide yard, glad of the sturdy shoes against the still-damp grass. The sun was warm on my shoulders and I held my cloak closed against the fitful wind. I went down the long gradual slope of the hill, the path twisting and turning with the ground's contours, until I was at the dark thicket of the woods.

The path narrowed but seemed well defined, following the course of least resistance, around trees and rocks, over natural hummocks where the land was boggy. I had forgotten the stagnant, heavy smell of the marsh, and now I wrinkled my nose as it enveloped me. The woods were dark and tangled, with the light behind me cut off after only a few turnings. The gloom closed about me and seemed very still; even the birds no longer called above me. Perhaps Becky had been right to suggest the road.

But I was half way, I was sure. It would be senseless to turn back, only to have to set out all over again.

My shoes squished on the soft ground, and I realized how swampy it had become. I picked my way carefully to stay on hard earth. Insects buzzed about my head and I waved my hands before me to keep them from my face. The path was less defined now, fading into marshy puddles or under the thick grass. The treacherous soft ground often looked exactly the same as the hard.

No wonder so many stories had grown up about the woods and marsh—it would be easy to let my imagination see all sorts of figures and menaces in the shadows. I wanted to run but I dared not. A misstep would tumble me into the treacherous pools of stagnant water and mud. Several times I had to grab branches or saplings to keep from pitching forward.

Had I taken a wrong turn, lost the path? I stopped and looked about, trying to identify the trail I had been following. The path had been so clear at first, it seemed impossible for it to have disappeared so suddenly.

A small sound startled me. A branch snapping . . . it was unmistakable! I peered around, searching the shadowy dimness, and caught a glimpse of movement. Frightened, I stifled a cry. Was it a bird jumping from branch to branch? There had been a flash of color, I was sure of it. I saw it a second time—and my instant impression was of a man, watching me, ducking out of sight as I turned unexpectedly in that direction.

"Who's there?" I called, barely above a whisper.

There was no answer and no further motion. The bit of color had vanished and the woods were still. I strained to hear any other sounds but none came. My own breath was harsh in my throat and my heart was pounding. Carefully, I picked my way toward the spot where the figure had been. I was frightened to investigate, but terrified not to. To my surprise, the spot was directly on the firm path—the one I'd missed somehow in turning. There was no sign of the silent watcher, or that he'd ever existed in anything but my imagination. I hurried along, sure of my footing now and wanting only to escape the woods as quickly as I could. The grotesque, twisted trunks of the ancient trees, the rank, untamed growth everywhere intimidated me. Shadows seemed to lengthen as I watched them, and the crawling vines moved as vagrant wisps of breeze fluttered branches they clung to. The path was soft with dead leaves, soggy from the recent rain, and my shoes made no sound. Had the watcher stolen away as softly?

I glanced back at every whisper of noise,

peering into the shadows and jumping at any motion. I had seen a man—I was sure of it. Even now, I felt the presence behind me. Someone was following me.

I breathed a sigh of relief as I saw the end of the woods ahead. The sunlight increased, the trees thinned, and the rank smell of the marsh gave way to fresh clean air as I emerged from the path and found myself in a sunny clearing that led to a gentle slope and Annie Newgate's cottage.

The house stood in a semi-circle of evergreens; it was gray stone, covered with trailing leafy vines that clawed the window panes and encroached the doorway. In summer, the entire cottage was buried under a mass of shiny greenery, which gave it a soft, pleasant appearance. But now, it was almost stark, with little to soften its rough lines. The flowerboxes along the windows were empty; only the curtains at the window gave any hint of color.

I walked up the path and lifted the brass knocker. The sound was loud, and I found myself straining to catch a response. When there was none, I rapped again, turning to look about the tiny yard while I waited.

A man came around the corner of the house, stopping to stare as he saw me. He was tall and wide-shouldered, wearing a plaid shirt that was rolled up at the sleeves. He was carrying an axe in his hands.

I felt uncomfortable and quickly broke the

silence. "I am Margaret Ashcroft. I've come to see Annie."

He continued to stare, his dark eyes studying me as though to learn all they could of me. He was a young man, under thirty, I was sure. His features were strong, yet pleasant—or would be if he smiled. He did not.

"She's abed. Not well, been ailing a long time." He shifted the axe and leaned it against the cottage wall.

"I'm sorry to hear that. But now that I've come this long way, may I at least speak to her?" I was not about to be turned away by this sullen young man, whoever he was. I was disheartened to hear that Annie was ill, but perhaps she might at least suggest something for Juliette.

He shrugged. "I'll see if she's awake." He walked to the cottage door and opened it, ducking his head to enter so he would not hit the lintel. I followed him quickly before he could bar my way. He said nothing, glancing back at me as he crossed to the curtained doorway at the rear of the tiny parlour.

I looked about. I had never been inside the cottage before, although I had driven here with my grandfather on several occasions. Annie lived in the house only a few years before I left Harrowgate, and my grandfather always considered her part of the household.

I heard the soft murmur of voices; moments later, the young man came back, shaking his head. "It will do no good to speak with her.

Her mind is wandering, as often it does."

He must have reacted to the expression of annoyance and disappointment on my face. He said, "But if you've a mind to, come ahead." He stepped aside and held back the curtain.

I walked into the tiny bedroom, barely large enough to contain the low rope bed and the tiny chest that filled it. The figure in the bed was more skeleton than human. Annie had always been frail in stature, but her illness had stretched the leathery skin over her bones so there seemed to be no flesh at all. Her wispy white hair stuck out in all directions, and her cheeks were sunken and hollow. She lay with eyes closed, and I could see the tracery of blue veins in the lids. Her thin shoulders were covered with a white flannel gown, longsleeved, and her bony fingers were twisted and gnarled.

She opened her eyes at the sound of our entry, dark pupils staring at the ceiling as her lips moved. Small sounds escaped her lips, a breath in the quiet room. They were a meaningless jumble, without words.

I moved to the bedside and bent over her. "Annie . . .? It's Margaret Ashcroft. You remember me, don't you? Margaret—?"

The gray eyes searched for the sound of my voice but did not focus on me. "Aaaahhh."

"Annie, the young lady's come all the way from the manor house to see you. Wants to talk to you, she does." The man's voice was strangely soothing to the old woman and she seemed to relax into the pillows. "There's a girl, now," he said. "Come now, say hello to Miss Margaret."

Annie's eyes found me then, and she stared intently. "Mr. Franklin never would do such a thing . . . he promised . . . always a place for old Annie—" The dry lips worked feverishly to get the words out. She was still staring at me but there was no recognition in her eyes. "The curse of Harrowgate. . . ."

The young man sighed heavily. "It's no use. You'd best come again another time, Miss."

I stood up, looking at him. "What did she mean about my grandfather?"

He shrugged. "It's common knowledge, I suppose. You'll be hearing it elsewhere, I'm sure."

"Then tell me."

He looked at me for a long moment, then said, "Your grandfather promised to see to Annie's needs for the rest of her life, but when his will was read, she had been cut out. A paltry few pounds, nothing more."

I could not have been more surprised if he had struck me. "But that's impossible—"

"It was done, none the less," he said grimly.

I understood his reluctance to let me see the old woman. No Ashcroft would be welcome here. "But why?" I asked.

He was silent, looking past me to the small rectangle of the window and the gray trees beyond. Then he said, "Village gossip holds that your grandfather fell under the curse of Harrowgate and that evil forces killed him."

"That's nonsense! He died of a heart attack—"

The young man glanced at me sidelong. "Yes. I know."

He was silent again until I finally asked, "Who are you?" He had not introduced himself; he seemed very much at home and very sure of himself.

For a moment I thought he did not intend to answer, but he said, "Name's Jonathon Newgate, Miss. Annie is my great-aunt. Guess I'm her only relative. I came over from Devonsworth to bring her the message when my father died, and found her like this. Couldn't leave her alone, so I just stayed on to tend her."

I had not known Annie had any relatives but his story was quite plausible. And he *was* taking care of her—someone had to do it, she was too feeble to care for herself.

He was watching me, and I grew uneasy once more. I had a brief thought of the man who'd watched me in the woods. Had it been Jonathon Newgate? If he was familiar with the path, he *could* have doubled back to the cabin to be here ahead of me.

"Was there something in particular you wanted of her?" Jonathon asked, indicating the old woman on the bed.

"Yes. Juliette is ill and wants Annie to tend her."

"Ah, that would be Miss Juliette Ilford, your brother's fiancée."

Surprised, I nodded. How did he know so much about the people of Harrowgate?

As though in answer to my question he said, "Annie has her lucid moments. She has spoken often of your grandfather's illness and how Juliette helped her care for him."

"Then you understand how important this is to Juliette now?"

"Has she been ill long?"

"Several weeks. I have just arrived but I am told she exhausted herself during my grandfather's illness. She is not a robust girl, and the winter has been hard on her."

"I see." He turned and left the room without a word.

Such a curious young man! I looked back to find Annie staring at me, her eyes glowing. "There is evil at Harrowgate," she whispered hoarsely. "The curse—death—"

I gasped, frightened by the intensity of her words and the feverish look in her eyes. Jonathon was in the doorway again and I stared at him.

"What is it—?"

"She was talking about death—" I could not control my shaking.

"Pay no heed. Her mind goes off on tangents and she lapses into the old ways."

"What do you mean?"

He glanced away. "Annie sees things, a sixth sense, you might say. She fancies she can predict the future."

I felt my pulse race. Predictions . . . I remembered my grandfather admonishing Annie not to indulge in such nonsense.

"And can she? Predict the future?" I asked.

He didn't answer immediately. "At times, Miss, at times." Abruptly, he changed the subject, holding up a dark bottle with a thick cork in it. "This is a tonic Annie had me prepare for her when I first came," he said. "She claims it has restorative powers for any illness. Miss Juliette might do well on it."

I accepted the bottle. "Thank you. I shall tell her Annie sent it herself. The power of suggestion may do as well to heal her as the mixture."

He looked offended, and I was sorry I had spoken so sharply, but his explanation of Annie's muttering had upset me. I glanced at the old woman; her eyes were closed again and she seemed to be asleep.

Jonathon moved out of the doorway to let me pass, then followed me across the parlour and out into the yard again. I thanked him once more and started toward the path.

"It would be best if you returned by way of the road, Miss."

"I have no carriage," I said shortly. I wanted to be away from him and the cottage, and I was too tired to consider the long route that would entail an hour or more of walking.

"If you can wait a bit, I can go to the next farm and borrow a wagon."

I shook my head. "That isn't necessary. It will only take me a short time to go back through the woods. I want to get the medicine to Juliette as soon as possible."

He grunted but said nothing more, and I felt his eyes on my back until I was out of sight along the path, the dark woods once more closing in behind me.

Why had I been so impatient? An hour would make no difference, and I certainly was not happy about the idea of making my way through the woods and marsh again. Already I felt the strange uneasiness the woods created—the feeling that I was not alone.

So far, my return to Harrowgate had not been joyous. I wished that Charles would hurry home and take charge. He had always been able to manage better than I. And Juliette would improve quickly once Charles was with her.

I grasped the bottle of elixir tightly and hurried along the path. It was easier to find now that I had travelled it once, but I could not shake the feeling of being watched. It was absurd, I told myself. I was quite alone. Who in the world would want to watch me? I offered no threat, held no secrets that might be discovered by spying. Surely Jonathon Newgate would not follow me.

As I gained the depths of the woods, the light was considerably dimmer, and my uneasiness grew. The path was slippery, and I had to slow down in order not to lose my way

again. The memory of my earlier mis-
adventure off the path was still clear in my
mind, and I shivered at the thought. I found
my breath coming in gasps, my heart racing. I
paused to lean against a gray tree bole and
catch my breath. The gnarled thing shifted, it
was a hollow skeleton. I clutched wildly at a
bush; nettles stung my palm and I brushed
them quickly as tears came to my eyes. In my
panic, I was making matters worse, and I
struggled to regain my composure. I moved
along the path again, unable to keep my feet
at a slow walk.

I stumbled and fell to one knee, crying out
as birds screamed and squawked at me
overhead, flapping away noisily. My temples
throbbed and my heart was hammering. I
slipped the bottle into the pocket of my cloak,
forcing myself to breathe deeply. If I fell I
might hurt myself and lie for hours before
anyone missed me and came looking for me.

Fear surrounded me as I forced myself to go
on. I could not let my fright grow to hysteria.
My knee was bruised from my fall and it
ached with each step. My foot slipped on the
wet ground, and I fell against a sagging limb
that creaked dangerously. It gave way with a
shivering crack as I clutched to keep myself
from sprawling. The grotesque length of it
crashed to the ground with a shuddering rum-
ble, narrowly missing my foot as I scurried
back. I went to my knees again, moaning as I
felt the skin lacerate.

I was thoroughly frightened now, confused. The woods were dark and the stench of the marsh clouded around me as the fallen branch stirred the brackish water. The woods seemed to rouse, to come horribly alive, resenting the intrusion. Birds screeched amid a great flapping of wings; a furry animal rustled in the undergrowth; and the wind flung a handful of dry evergreen needles spewing at my face.

I stumbled to my feet, sobbing. I had to get out of this place—I *had* to! The sounds around me were loud, like someone crashing toward me. I screamed as I thought of the man I was sure had watched me earlier. Was he stalking me, waiting to pounce?

Annie's words whispered in my ears . . . "There's evil at Harrowgate . . . death. . . ."

I bolted, fleeing blindly, fighting my way out of the thicket, stumbling and crawling, pulling myself erect. Surely he was right behind me—I could hear the heavy sound of his steps snapping dead branches, rustling thick leaves.

I could scarcely breathe, so great was my fright. I cried out, sobbing. A huge shadow appeared on the path in front of me, dark and menacing. I screamed and felt the gray terror envelop me as I slid to the ground, collapsing in a faint.

Chapter Six

Consciousness returned slowly. I opened my eyes and stared at the shredded clouds against the blue sky. I could smell the damp grass; above me the trees swayed in the breeze and birds trilled their songs. I felt curiously distant, as though seeing the world from a far-off place.

Then reality returned, and with it the memory of the figure that had frightened me. I sat up, looking about wildly, almost expecting to find myself in the swamp with the mysterious stranger hovering over me, threatening . . .

But I was quite alone. I was no longer in the woods but on the grass of the meadow. Safe— I stared at the hill glistening in the sun. Beyond a fringe of tall elms, I could see the turrets of the house, the occasional glint of sun on a windowpane.

I turned to look at the woods. From this safe distance, they seemed almost benign.

How had I gotten here? How could I have run out of the woods and reached the meadow? I remembered nothing except my stark terror and the swirling darkness that had engulfed me into oblivion. Surely I could not have made my own way through the treacherous swamp and not recall it!

Puzzled, I rose to my feet, looking about in search of an explanation. Someone had brought me here, there was no other way it could have happened. But who? And why had he not waited? I thought about the dark shadow on the path. Who had it been? If the attempt to frighten me had been deliberate, why had the stranger then rescued me and carried me to safety?

I shook my head, gazing back at the woods. It didn't make sense, but my relief was so enormous that nothing else mattered. I brushed myself free of grass and twigs and smoothed my skirt. I felt at the pocket of my cloak and discovered that the bottle of medicine was unbroken. With a sigh of relief, I started up the hill.

No one was about in the hall as I entered the house, and I was grateful for the chance to slip upstairs and clean up before I had to face anyone. Had someone from the house found me and carried me from the woods? It seemed unlikely, but so many strange things had taken place since my arrival at Harrowgate, I no longer was sure of anything.

In my room, I washed, then sponged the mud spots from my skirt. There were several long scratches on my face where brambles had torn at my skin; I tried to disguise them with powder but was not altogether successful.

As I brushed my cloak and hung it away, my gaze was drawn to the shelf—the green shawl was gone. How very strange . . . Becky had professed no knowledge of it. Had Emma Mundy come to claim it?

Sighing, I closed the wardrobe and picked up the bottle of medicine. I crossed the hall and tapped gently on Juliette's door. I thought I heard a whisper of sound inside but no one called out to me. I turned the knob and pushed the door open.

Juliette was awake, staring at the door with wide, frightened eyes. She looked relieved as she recognized me. I went to the bed, displaying the bottle I had brought.

"I have just come from Annie!" I said, smiling. "The storm has caused her arthritis to flare up and she finds it difficult to get about." No sense alarming her with the seriousness of the old woman's condition. "She sent this, said it will have you right in no time."

I set the bottle on the table and looked about for a measure to pour a dose. Juliette's gaze followed me about the room. When I turned to her again, she tried to smile.

"I will be well now that you have come, Margaret, I know I will."

"Of course you shall. Here now, take this." She opened her mouth dutifully and I spooned the liquid into it.

She lay back, more relaxed than I had seen

her since my arrival. Still, a worried line etched between her brows.

"Margaret, as soon as I am well enough, will you take me away?"

Her words surprised me and I looked at her intently. "Away? From Harrowgate?"

She nodded. "There is evil here . . ."

Annie had uttered the same words . . . Puzzled, I asked, "I realize the strain of my grandfather's illness has been hard on you. If you'd written—but too late for that now. Of course, you may leave Harrowgate whenever you wish, but what of Charles? He'll expect you to be here when he returns."

Her eyes grew distant and tears welled. "Charles . . ."

"You must not worry because his letters are delayed. The voyage to and from the Cape is long."

She looked at me imploringly. "I have not heard from him since he brought me here!" she said, tightening her fingers on my arm. "Oh, Margaret, I have been sick with worry. He promised to write as soon as he returned to London, then during the journey—" The tears spilled over.

"There now, crying won't help. The mails are unreliable, perhaps his letters went astray."

Charles had been gone more than four months. I could understand her concern. It was unlike him not to keep his promise, especially when he knew she would worry.

"Do you really think he will come?" Her expression was hopeful.

"Of course. The mails may be unreliable, but Charles is not." I smiled and brushed a wisp of hair away from her cheek. "He will be here soon to surprise you."

That seemed to comfort her and she relaxed again. "I am so glad you've come," she repeated. "I do feel better already, really I do."

"Fine. Now rest and gain strength. Perhaps tomorrow we can sit in the garden if the sun is warm. It will be summer soon, the air grows warmer each day."

"Yes, I'd like that."

I left her and made my way to the lower floor, meeting Becky at the foot of the wide marble stairway. She was carrying a tray, and bobbed a curtsy at me.

"Lunch is being served, Miss. I've a tray for Miss Juliette."

"I've just left her. Please see that she rests after she eats."

"Yes'm."

The others were seated at the table when I entered. Wiley pushed back his chair, unfolding his lean frame and standing back so he could pull one out for me. I thanked him and sat as the Mundys stared at me. I was aware of the scratches on my face that I had been unable to hide with powder.

"What in the world happened to you?" Lionel asked.

I made light of it. "I stumbled in the woods."

Emma shuddered. "Those woods are dangerous, you shouldn't be wandering around there."

"I wasn't wandering about. I went to see Annie."

She nodded but her expression didn't change.

Wiley said, "Did you find the old woman at home?"

"Yes. Bedridden, as a matter of fact."

"Old and feeble minded," Lionel said decisively. "Waste of time trying to talk to her." He looked at me questioningly.

I found myself being irritated with him once more. What was it about him that put me ill at ease so quickly? I didn't want to believe it was the fact that he had been a servant and I still regarded him as such. That would be unfair when the Mundys had done so much to keep Harrowgate running during my grandfather's illness and now Juliette's.

I realized he was repeating a question. "Did you talk to her?"

"For a moment. As you say, her mind wanders. She babbled about a curse and death."

Emma looked upset. "Crazy old woman. Ought to be put away in an institution."

"She seems quite harmless," I said. "And with her nephew to care for her, she seems to do all right."

"He's still there then? Jonathon . . . ?" Wiley said.

"Yes." I wondered why no one had mentioned Jonathon to me if they were aware of his being at the cottage. Jonathon had told me he'd come to find his great-aunt too ill to care for herself. That meant he'd been there awhile, yet neither the Mundys nor Wiley Temple had thought to mention that Annie was bedridden before I set out to visit her. I dismissed the thought. Everything these people did seemed confusing.

"It seems strange to me, Mr. Temple, that my grandfather did not leave any bequest to Annie," I said. They looked at me, startled. I went on. "Annie seemed quite upset by it."

"Please, call me Wiley." He smiled and I forgot my uneasiness momentarily. "Your grandfather left her a hundred pounds. I'd hardly call that nothing."

"But he always spoke of pensioning her for life. The cottage—did he make no arrangements for it to be deeded to her?"

"I'm afraid not," Wiley said. "It's been my experience that people often say one thing and do quite another when it comes right down to it. Perhaps your grandfather considered such a bequest, then changed his mind. He might have been dissatisfied with Annie for some reason."

I found that difficult to believe, but there was no point in arguing a dead man's intentions. Perhaps when Charles returned, he

71

could rectify our grandfather's oversight and provide for Annie.

Lionel sat back and stared at me. "We thought it best to let Annie stay on at the cottage, even though no arrangements had been made. It isn't as if it could be rented out—"

"I wouldn't think of having her put out!" I said.

He construed it as an acknowledgement of his wisdom. "I told Mr. Temple you'd feel that way."

I glanced at Wiley but let the matter drop there.

In the silence that followed, I became aware of the steady, mournful sound of a distant church bell. A vague memory stirred as I tried to place the meaning of it and could not. I asked about it.

Lionel shrugged. "A death, I suppose. The rector at the village church seems determined to share bad news with the countryside."

"One of the old people, I suspect," Emma said. "Seems one passes on every week or two."

The brass knocker on the front door sounded so suddenly that we all jumped. Lionel frowned, getting to his feet and hurrying from the room. Wiley turned to watch him, and was still staring at the door when Lionel returned a few moments later with the village constable.

"There's been a death—"

"What is it, Constable?" Wiley demanded.

"How does it concern us?"

"Begging your pardon, sir, a body's been discovered in the woods here at Harrowgate."

Emma dropped her spoon and it clattered against the cup. Her eyes were wide and frightened.

"Who is—was—it?" She could scarcely get the words out.

The constable shook his head. "A stranger, ma'am. No one seems to recognize him. Judging by his papers, his name is Simpson and he is from London."

"How awful!" I felt a shiver run through me. My mind whirled with thoughts of the terror I had felt in the woods, and the overpowering feeling that I was being watched or followed. Could it have been this man, Simpson?

"How—how did he die?" I managed to ask.

The constable hesitated, then said, "Died in the marsh, ma'am."

I shuddered and made a small sound. The horror of my own experience seemed all the more dreadful for knowing that someone else had not fared as well.

"Body's been there some weeks, the doctor says."

I wasn't sure if that relieved my fears or not. There was small comfort in knowing I might have passed within yards of the body—even stumbled on it!

"Are you all right, Miss? You look pale." The constable frowned.

"Yes . . . it's just that I was in the woods this morning. When I think I might have—"

"How was the body discovered, constable? It's a bit unusual for the local police to be wandering around in Harrowgate woods," Wiley asked with an insinuating look.

"We had a report, sir. A young artist who's leased the Rutherford cottage found it. He'd gone for a walk and didn't realize the woods were private property."

I found my voice again. "This young man was in the woods this morning then?"

"Yes, Miss. Came directly to the station in Louthwick to report it. Our people are just removing the body now. I was sent here to ask if any of you can help in identifying him."

Lionel shook his head. "I've never heard of anyone named Simpson, and we haven't seen any strangers about."

The constable nodded. "A few people in the village recall a stranger a few weeks back. Man asking questions. Seemed very interested in one thing."

"And what was that, Constable?" Wiley asked.

"Harrowgate, sir. The man asked a lot of questions about Harrowgate."

I felt another shiver rake through me. Why would anyone be interested in this place—was there any link between the man's curiosity and his death? I didn't want to think about it. I wondered if I should mention the figures I'd seen last night on the drive. I was no longer sure they had been real. Now I was completely unnerved by the episode in the woods, and I dared not mention my fears aloud. I would be considered a hysterical female who saw danger in every shadow.

"Seems the man might have come to Harrowgate for a purpose," the constable said.

"That's nonsense," Lionel said sharply. "We would know if anyone had been snooping about. Whatever his business was, he never came here to state it."

"I see. Thank you, sir. These questions have to be asked," the constable said almost apologetically.

"We understand," Wiley said, rising and sliding his hand under the constable's arm to turn him about and usher him from the room. The man nodded to me, then followed Wiley out.

As the murmur of their voices faded, I shivered again. I felt Lionel and Emma Mundy staring at me but I could not meet their gaze. My mind whirled with the realization that Annie Newgate had predicted death—and death had come to Harrowgate!

I finished the food on my plate in silence. I wondered what the Mundys were thinking, for I felt their eyes on me with every bite. I was ill at ease, and I did not meet their curious stares. It was almost as though they were accusing me, linking my journey through the woods with this strange new development. I wished Wiley would come back, but when he did not, after a decent interval I excused myself and left to go upstairs. To my surprise, Wiley was waiting for me in the hall.

"Margaret, don't let this upset you," he said gently. He took my arm and walked with me upstairs. I wondered if he didn't want the Mundys to overhear—and I wondered, too, at the warm sense of pleasure his touch gave me. My cheeks felt warm, and I prayed that I was not blushing.

"I'm dreadfully sorry about all this. I wish there were some way I could spare you." He smiled and his dark eyes seemed to search beyond my thoughts. "Are you quite sure you were not hurt more seriously than you've admitted in your mishap in the woods?"

"I'm fine," I assured him. I had an impulse to tell him how frightened I had been, and how curious I still was about who had rescued me so opportunely, but somehow I could not bring myself to it. If Wiley had been the one, surely he would admit it. And if not him— who? Certainly not the Mundys—or Jonathon Newgate. Their hostility was so obvious, I doubted any of them would care if I perished in the swamp!

At my door, Wiley paused, his hand still on my arm. "You're sure you're all right?" he said again, his gaze lingering on me protectively.

I knew then I was blushing, and I lowered my gaze. "Yes, I'm perfectly all right, but I do feel a little bit foolish. I realize now I'm letting old memories haunt me. So much of my life here at Harrowgate was unhappy that I'm seeing menace at every turn."

Gently, he raised his hand to touch my cheek. "No one here wants to harm you," he said. "We're all delighted you are back." His fingertips lingered at the long scratch on my cheek. "Especially me."

His last words were spoken so softly, I told myself I had not heard right. For a long moment, we stood gazing at each other. My pain and fright evaporated as I responded to his gentle touch. It had been so long—

Self-consciously, I said, "Thank you, Wiley. I know that is true. . . ." My pulse raced madly and my breath caught in a fiery coil in my chest.

"Good," he said after what seemed like a very long time. "If you need anything, or there's anything I can do, my room is there." He indicated the door just next to mine. His hand left my flesh reluctantly.

Too confused to answer, I gave him a final smile and went into my room. As I closed the door, I stood a moment with my back to it, remembering the incredibly gentle touch of his caressing fingers.

Chapter Seven

I spent the afternoon sitting with Juliette, reading aloud to her and, when the afternoon sun was at its peak, coaxing her from her bed and letting her sit in the wing chair near the window. Perhaps it was the excitement of having someone take over responsibility, but I was sure there was a touch of color in her cheeks. Juliette gave credit to Annie Newgate's potion.

At dinner time, I asked Becky to bring me a tray and I dined with Juliette in companionable silence. She was tired from her busy day, and I knew she would sleep well. I had carefully avoided mentioning anything that might upset her, keeping her mind on cheerful thoughts so neither of us would have time to brood.

When at last she was tucked in for the night, I retired to my own room without going downstairs. I had no desire to spoil the pleasantness of the afternoon with somber thoughts that seemed to abound when I was with the Mundys, as much as I would have enjoyed Wiley's company. Juliette had not asked about the church bells, and I had not brought up the subject of the dead man in the woods.

But I had not succeeded in banishing it completely from my thoughts. The idea of having been so close to a corpse left me with a chill. And what of the man I'd glimpsed? I was convinced of his reality now. Had it been the artist who discovered the body? Why had he not spoken to me or made his presence known?

The events of the day had exhausted me, and I found myself nodding over the book I'd brought up from the library. The sky outside was dark and the house was silent. I'd seen Becky hurrying down the drive as dusk fell, glancing behind her as though she expected to see a pursuing ghost.

During the years I had lived at Harrowgate, I'd heard tales of the haunted east wing. Grandfather Franklin refused to discuss them, shushing Charles and me whenever we asked. Several times, prodded by Charles' daring, we had ventured into the shut-up portion of the house, walking on tiptoes and jumping at every sound. I'd forced myself to follow my brother through the dusty rooms on up the creaking stairs. The furniture had been left in place when the wing was closed, and mice had chewed the upholstery so that stuffing spilled in untidy heaps to the floor and trailed about. In spite of Charles' active imagination we had seen no ghosts. But we had found something else—or he had. In the huge ballroom that had covered the ground floor, Charles had discovered a loose panel at one side of the raised dias from which the orchestra had once played. Pulling it free, he crawled under the stage and coaxed me to follow. It was dark and dusty and full of cobwebs, but he was delighted with it and called it our den—our tiger's den. Once Annie had caught us and chased us from the ballroom, warning us it was not safe.

How long ago that seemed. . . .

I rose from the chair and walked to the window to draw back the curtain and stare across the dark yard toward the east wing. The figure I'd seen last night had gone in that direction. Was someone there? Hiding, perhaps? But why?

I could find no answers, so I resolutely blanked the thoughts from my mind as I prepared for bed. The shadows seemed to bring with them somber thoughts and frightening possibilities—and I wanted to wish away the hours of darkness and see the sun again. Tomorrow I would ask Wiley the exact terms of my grandfather's will. If any bequest had been left to me, I might be able to do something for Annie before Charles got home. I could not understand why Charles had not kept his promise to write to Juliette. It wasn't like him to worry someone he so obviously loved.

I fell asleep thinking of Charles and his

mysterious silence. I dreamed of storms at sea and the dreadful war that had taken him to South Africa.

I awoke, struggling, with labored breath, aware that I had been deep in a nightmare. Sitting up in bed, I stared at the gloom until I recognized the dim outlines of furniture and realized where I was. Once again I saw the portrait across the room in the eerie reflected moonlight, and the girl again looked incredibly sad. Strange how the light affected the picture—or my eyes viewing it.

I judged it to be about three in the morning, and the house was silent around me, everyone asleep. No—the house was not silent. I held my breath, listening. What was it—a curious low sound? A soft murmur, as if someone were talking in a low voice, far away, the sound muffled by walls.

I sat motionless, wondering who it could be. Who would be up and about, conversing at this hour? I couldn't even be sure the sound came from inside the house. Remembering the figures on the lawn the night before, I threw back the covers and donned robe and slippers. I went to the window and eased back the drape so I could look down on the drive. I could see no one. Curious, I forgot the nightmare and my own fears and crossed to the door, standing a moment with my ear to it to listen again. The voice was more distinct but I still could not make out words. I bit my lip, opening the door slowly, ready to pull back inside at the slightest indication I'd been seen.

The sound of the mysterious voices was louder; they seemed to be coming from the foyer at the foot of the stairs. I knew I should go back to bed and put it out of my mind, but curiosity impelled me forward—there were so many things about Harrowgate I wanted to know. I felt responsible until Charles returned, and I had a right to know what was going on. As I moved through the darkness, my steps were soundless on the carpeted hall, but I was tense with suppressed excitement at my own daring.

Each of the doors I passed was closed, and no light showed under any of them. I had not inquired which rooms the Mundys occupied. Wiley's door was dark, as was Juliette's. I felt slightly foolish prowling about in the dark.

A faint bluish light illuminated the hall toward the front of the house. I paused at the balcony that overlooked the foyer. The light did not come from there but from above, and I suddenly recalled the small alcove with a leaded glass window that looked onto the drive where it curved toward the east wing. Mesmerized, I moved toward it. Spectral moonlight glowed through the window, falling along the end of the hall like a blue path. A cloud moved across the moon, and the hallway was suddenly dark.

I could hear the murmuring voices more clearly now—two people talking in very hushed tones. The sound came from below. I moved to the balustrade and peered down.

A very faint glow, no more than a breath of silvery illumination, filmy as a floating cobweb, spilled across the foyer from the tall windows at either side of the main entrance door. I stared into the darkness as I tried to identify shadows and locate the source of the voices. They were somewhat muffled, as if behind a door. I realized they had to be coming from the library that opened off the main hall, but there was no slash of brightness to indicate lamplight inside the room. I considered going down, but I could not bring myself to burst in on whoever was there. If Wiley or Lionel had some nocturnal business, it was really no concern of mine. Any pretense I might invent would be totally transparent. Resolutely, I turned to go back to my room, but I was startled by the sound of a door opening. I froze, not knowing which way to turn. The shadows below me stirred as two figures emerged from the library and crossed the hall. I could not make out their faces but there was no mistaking Wiley's tall, thin figure. I pressed against the wall, hoping I was invisible in the event one of them looked up.

The front door opened and a draft of cold air eddied up the stairwell around my feet. The second man slipped outside. Wiley closed the door softly behind him. For a moment, panic assailed me. If Wiley came upstairs and caught me listening I would feel ridiculous. I blushed at the thought. I was vastly relieved when Wiley disappeared along the lower hall. I let my breath out slowly as my heart raced. Once again I started for my room, but I paused to glance at the alcove window. I was unable to stem my curiosity. The window would give me a view of the drive and I might see where the mysterious night visitor went. Standing on tiptoe, I gazed down to the yard below.

The moon was out again, bathing the driveway in a silvery glow. There was a quick movement as a dark form detached itself from the clinging shadows and moved across the path. It was a man, but it was too dark to see more than his stocky silhouette. He walked casually and seemed very sure of himself. There was no fumbling in his choice of direction as he cut across the drive, skirting the flower borders with their freshly turned earth, and headed toward the east wing.

A thousand questions raced through my mind. Who was he? He seemed so at home, his pace casual and not at all furtive. He was certainly not a burglar if Wiley admitted him to the house. And Wiley and the Mundys had stated emphatically to the constable that there had been no strangers around Harrowgate . . . Yet if he were a guest, why was it necessary to stay hidden?

I watched as he reached the far side of the lawn and disappeared into the deeper shadows of the east wing. I stared long after he vanished to see if a light would appear, but none did. Where had he gone?

Slowly, I became aware of another sound, something quite close. I turned with a start, expecting Wiley had somehow come up the stairs without my hearing him. But it was not him.

I gasped aloud in astonishment, fighting the impulse to scream! There, coming along the hallway was the girl in the portrait—Elizabeth Ashcroft!

My hands were icy and I pressed back into the alcove, gripping the cold sill of the window. The figure moved toward me, humming softly. That was the sound I'd heard. The girl made no other noise as she moved along the hall. She seemed to ignore me completely, looking straight ahead, smiling as though absorbed in some secret thought.

I wanted to run, but I knew my legs would not carry me. The girl was so real, yet she was not real; she was not filmy or transparent, but yet not solid. I wanted to examine my feelings about the phenomenon but my brain would not function. My mind recalled the man I'd seen the night before—the figure that had seemed to move right through the closed door.

The apparition moved closer. It could not be a living being. This was not someone dressed in a costume, this was a phantom of the past. My terrified mind would not let me use the word 'ghost.'

The figure—the spectre—was humming a soft, lilting tune, and she was smiling. She was almost abreast of me, yet she gave no indication that she noticed my presence. The faint odor of rosewater drifted to me as the figure passed. I thought I could hear the whisper of the girl's voluminous skirts as she moved. Overlaying my terror was the feeling that I was in no real danger. The girl seemed to radiate happiness, her face and dark eyes shining.

I noticed then that she carried a small brass-bound chest in her hands. Carefully, almost lovingly. The figure moved to the stairs and began to descend, still humming softly.

I found I had been holding my breath, and now I let it out with relief. My knees were shaking and my thumping heart began to slow. My first instinct was to run to my room and once more burrow under the covers to hide from any such visions, but my curiosity grew with each second. The girl had not harmed me, not even noticed me.

Where was she going? What was she about?

With conscious decision, I moved to the head of the stairs, peering over the rail and glimpsing the wraith-like figure as it crossed the foyer below, moving into the deep shadows. With one hand on the balustrade, I hurried down the steps, determined to keep the girl in sight.

I moved quickly, but not carefully enough. Halfway down, my slipper caught in the hem of my dressing gown and I felt myself pitch forward into the darkness, the hard stairs came up before me. I screamed—my head struck stone—and I plummeted into blackness.

Chapter Eight

I regained consciousness to find myself lying on a couch in the parlour. Emma Mundy was bending over me, pressing a cold cloth to my head. As I opened my eyes, Emma sighed and dabbed at my face.

"She's coming around . . ."

It took me a moment to identify the voice, then I saw Lionel Mundy standing behind his wife, a worried frown creasing his brow.

I blinked and tried to clear my mind but it was still a blur. My shoulder ached and I could feel a painful lump under the cloth Emma pressed to my forehead.

"You're all right now," she said. "Gave us quite a scare, you did."

Then I remembered falling down the stairs as I tried to follow the vanishing figure of the ghost-girl. I tried to sit up, and felt a quick stab of pain in my ankle. I winced and Emma frowned again.

"Best you lie still awhile. You took a nasty fall."

Lionel scowled. "Those stone steps are treacherous. You could have been killed."

I shivered at his ominous tone and closed my eyes for a moment. When I opened them, Wiley was kneeling beside me, holding out a glass. "Drink this," he encouraged. "It will help you feel better." He slipped an arm about my shoulders and raised my head. His long fingers clasped over mine as I took the glass shakily. He gave me a coaxing smile.

The sharp warmth of the brandy shocked me, but he held the glass at my lips until I had taken another sip. When he lowered my head to the cushions, I could already feel myself relaxing. I smiled to thank him.

"What happened?" he asked gently. We might have been alone in the room for all the attention he paid the scowling Mundys, who stood at the end of the couch like two dark sentinels.

I hesitated. I wanted to tell him everything, but with the Mundys gaping in disapproval, I could not admit the story about the girl. They had already hinted that my imagination was too active. I had no desire to open myself to their ridicule again.

"I tripped on the stairs," I said finally.

"Such a racket." Emma Mundy sniffed. "We found you crumpled at the bottom of the steps."

"What in the world were you doing wandering about the house in the middle of the night?" Lionel demanded.

His attitude was infuriating, but I bit my lip and sat up. My ankle sent a sharp lace of pain up my leg at the movement, and I winced. Wiley was instantly solicitous.

"What is it?"

"I must have turned my ankle . . ."

Emma bent to examine my foot, while Wiley patted my hand reassuringly.

"It's beginning to swell," Emma pronounced. "It's probably sprained. Get another ice pack, Lionel." She looked at me sternly. "Best you lie down again and keep that foot up. It will help keep the swelling down."

Wiley quickly plumped the pillow and lowered me onto it. Emma brought another and propped it under the throbbing ankle. Another jolt of pain shot up my leg.

Lionel returned with a heavy towel folded over crushed ice. When he'd handed it to Emma, he stood staring at me from the foot of the couch. "Sleepwalking can be very dangerous," he said in a low growl.

With annoyance, I glanced at him. "I was not sleepwalking," I retorted with some heat.

"If you weren't sleepwalking, what *were* you doing?" he persisted.

I did not answer until Emma had placed the icy cold pack on my ankle and adjusted it to her satisfaction. The pain began to numb quickly.

"What were you doing?" Lionel demanded again.

I snapped, heedless of the consequences, "I heard voices and went to investigate!"

He was startled at first, then peered at me

warily. For a moment, I detected rage in his eyes, but he masked it quickly. His tone was derisive. "*Voices?* Everyone was in bed until you screamed loud enough to wake us. Hummph. I'd say you were dreaming, young lady."

"I was not dreaming!" I dared not look at Wiley, but I prayed he would come to my rescue. Why didn't he substantiate my story? Finally I said, "There were voices—and I saw someone leave the house and walk to the east wing."

Wiley was still silent, and I immediately regretted my outburst. If he'd had a secret meeting with someone in the library, it was obvious he didn't want the Mundys to know about it. I sensed his displeasure as he rose from his knees and stood looking down at me.

"There was no one here," Lionel said emphatically. "No one at all. It must have been a dream."

Emma nodded and shifted the cold compress on my ankle. She and her husband were presenting a solid front against me, and for some reason I did not understand, Wiley did not broach it. The room was very quiet for several moments as they waited for me to admit my error. I could not bring myself to lie.

"I saw him," I insisted. "He left the house and walked down the drive. He was quite clear in the moonlight for several seconds."

Wiley spoke at last. "Where were you when you saw him so well?"

91

Hesitantly, I pointed toward the stairs. "Up there, at the little window in the alcove."

"I see. Then you came down to investigate?"

Without thinking, I answered quickly. "No, I followed the girl—" I blurted the words before I realized they were out.

All three faces turned to me in astonishment.

"What girl?" Emma asked. "There's no one here but yourself and Juliette, and she certainly isn't well enough to be wandering about in the night."

"The girl in the portrait." There was no retreating now that I had gone this far. "The portrait in my room—Elizabeth Ashcroft."

Emma's face paled and she clasped her hands to her breast, forgetting the ice pack at my ankle so it slipped to the cushions and she had to retrieve it quickly. "Elizabeth Ashcroft—?! She's dead—!"

Lionel grunted. "You're telling us you saw a ghost?" He shook his head as though trying to placate a disturbed child.

"I did see her," I insisted. "She was walking along the hall. When she came downstairs, I followed her. That's when I fell."

I looked from one to another of them challengingly. Their expressions were amazed and skeptical. Lionel looked disgusted with me.

"My dear child," he said patronizingly, "Elizabeth Ashcroft died ages ago, long before

92

any of us came to Harrowgate to live."

"I saw her just the same." The belligerence was gone from my voice. I knew how foolish it sounded, and once more I regretted speaking so hastily. It would have been better to be silent about the ghostly apparition.

Wiley moved so he was in my line of vision. He smiled reassuringly. "It might be well for Lionel to take you into the village in the morning to see the doctor. Perhaps he can prescribe a sedative—"

"I don't need a sedative," I protested. The suggestion that it was my mind that needed doctoring angered me.

Soothingly, Wiley said, "At least let him look at your ankle. We don't want you to be hobbling about and perhaps taking another fall."

I sighed and closed my eyes. There was little point in arguing with him. I could not make up my mind whether his concern was genuine or merely an attempt to get my mind off what had happened. At last I murmured that I would see how my foot felt in the morning, and it seemed to satisfy him. The more I contemplated the idea, the less resistance I found to it. The doctor could answer my questions about my grandfather's death. Had it been his heart, or was there some foundation to Annie's mumblings about the curse of Harrowgate—unnatural forces?

I lay with the ice on my ankle a while longer, then Emma bound it tightly with a cloth. When I made a feeble attempt to get up, Wiley was at my side instantly. He scooped me from the couch and cradled me in his arms. I had no choice but to put my arms around his neck and cling to him. I was keenly aware of the faint odor of his shaving soap and the strength of his arms. My cheeks colored.

With a smile, he said, "That foot is in no condition to bear your weight yet. Give it the rest it requires." He swept me past the Mundys and started up the stairs. Lionel muttered in a low tone, but I could not hear his words. Emma quickly picked up a lamp and hurried after us.

The shadows leaped and danced eerily, but I blessed the dimness that kept Wiley from seeing how his nearness flustered me. He pushed open the door to my room with his foot. Inside, he waited until Emma set the lamp on the table, then lowered me gently to the bed. He tucked the covers around me, first making sure they were not tight across my injured foot. When he arranged them over my shoulders, his face was so close I felt his breath on my cheek.

Emma fussed but finally went out, leaving us alone. I smiled gratefully at Wiley.

"Thank you." I wanted to ask him about his assignation in the library, but my tongue was strangely tied. He was an enigma—silent and remote one moment, gentle and warm the next. I had never known anyone like him. At times he was as mysterious as the Mundys. I was thoroughly confused and no longer trusted my judgment.

He gave the cover a final pat and smiled. "If you need anything during the night, call. I'll be sure to hear." He gazed at me a moment, then said, "Promise you will not go wandering about anymore?" His eyes were black velvet as he watched me and waited for an answer.

"I promise."

"Good. Now sleep well, Margaret. . . ."

He moved slowly and I saw him as though in a dream. His face hovered over mine, and then his lips brushed mine like the touch of a butterfly in flight. The warm flood of pleasure that filled me banished my surprise until it was too late to react. Without looking back, he let himself out and the door closed quietly behind him.

Despite the warm quilt, I was trembling and my heart raced. I tried to tell myself I was reading far too much into a gesture of kindness. Or was it pity? Did he still think I was the confused dreaming sleepwalker the Mundys had accused me of being? Or was his gentle kiss a way of saying he believed my story? He knew part of it to be true . . . maybe he was accepting all of it.

I glanced at the portrait of Elizabeth Ashcroft. She was placid and smiling. Sighing, I blew out the lamp and settled to sleep for what was left of the night.

In the morning, I felt rested and all my gloomy thoughts had vanished. I stepped gingerly as I got out of bed, testing my ankle cautiously. It twinged slightly, but I could walk with only a bit of a limp. It was a minor sprain, I was sure. The icepack and firm bandage had kept the swelling to a minimum. It would be as good as new in a few days. I dressed and went downstairs to breakfast.

The others were already done and the table was cleared. I had slept soundly when I settled down and it was much later than my usual hour for rising. I found the cook, Mrs. Dobbs, in the kitchen. She insisted it was no trouble to fix me something. I said I would eat in the kitchen and sat at the wide table where the sun warmed my back. Becky Riker came through from the scullery with an armload of mops and brooms. She smiled shyly, but said nothing. I noted her quick glance at my bandaged foot. I suspected Emma had mentioned my mishap and probably suggested that I had been sleepwalking.

Mrs. Dobbs set a plate of coddled eggs and sausage before me. One a separate dish, piping hot scones sent up a delectable aroma that made my mouth water, and a small pot of strawberry jam and a little crock of creamery butter. Suddenly I was ravenous.

From time to time, Mrs. Dobbs glanced at me but she did not engage me in conversation. I was content to eat in silence and enjoy the warm sunshine. When I had just about finished the last delicious scone, Lionel entered. He seemed surprised to see me there.

"Are you well enough to be up?" he asked.

"Yes, but I think I will see the doctor to be on the safe side. Is there a carriage I can use?"

"I'll take you myself," he said.

"That isn't necessary, if you've a light rig." I had driven grandfather's carriages many times. And I was not overjoyed at the prospect of the ride to the village in Lionel's dour company.

He frowned but said he would bring the carriage around in half an hour.

I used the time to look in on Juliette, asking her if there was anything I might bring her. She said not, and I promised to sit with her upon my return. She actually looked improved this morning; her eyes had lost much of the dullness and a faint blush of color touched her cheeks.

It was an exceptional day. There were a few clouds, but the sky was a brilliant blue and the air perfect. I was glad of the chance to be out. Ever since my arrival at Harrowgate, I had felt oppressed by the atmosphere of the old house, and now the thought of getting away from it for awhile was part of my enjoyment.

The chestnut horse stepped lightly as I flicked the reins, and the phaeton moved down the drive. The open-sided carriage let the warm air blow over me and the canopy kept the sun from my eyes. I felt invigorated and let the horse have his head as I glanced about at the countryside. The hills were green and new leaves rustled on the branches of the trees.

Near the foot of the hill, the road wound through the edge of the woods, the shade closing about the carriage like welcoming arms. The air seemed more hushed here, as though the somber mood of the woods tried to reach out and envelope the road, but without success. There was nothing ominous about the trees; they lay dappled in the sunshine, alive with the chirping of birds and the promise of summer. How very different from the terrifying darkness they'd held yesterday as I dashed headlong through the marsh!

The chestnut whinnied and quickened its pace as though sensing my remembered terror. I sat up, glancing about and realized that this was the spot where I'd seen the strange frightening figure of the white-bearded old man in the road when the coach had brought me to Harrowgate. There was nothing now, yet I shivered. Had the figure been warning me? Waving me back? Wiley insisted that he had not seen it, nor had the coachman. That had been the beginning; since then I had seen other ghostly figures—the man with the dagger and Elizabeth Ashcroft, the girl of the picture. I had never seen a ghost before in my life, now suddenly I had been confronted by three in a short space of time. Why?

I had given little thought to the supernatural nor had I examined my feelings about it. Despite what I'd seen, I wasn't at all sure that I believed in ghosts. I would have thought they clanked about in chains, haunting old castles.

I brushed aside the thoughts as the carriage emerged from the woods and came into the sunlight again. As the road reached the valley, it straightened out and the turns became more gradual. I looked out over the rolling fields, freshly plowed and planted. I could see distant figures bent in labor over furrows; and a man stood, hand at his back, watching the carriage pass.

The road forked, with one branch curving along the base of the hill toward the east and winding back into the valley where Annie Newgate's cottage nestled. The other made a more direct path to Louthwick; the horse chose it without direction.

The village had not changed in the years I'd been gone. The few shops and businesses were clustered along the main street, with hitching posts at the edge of the walkway. Several carriages and wagons were tied at various points, and men and boys bustled about loading supplies. The white steeple of the church spired into the blue sky, the bell now silent. Women strolled, looking in shop windows, pausing to chat. Heads turned in my direction as I brought the phaeton up before the gray clapboard building where Doctor Foxx had his consulting rooms.

A woman in dark calico and a white apron and stiffly starched cap opened the door, ushering me to a waiting room while she went to tell the doctor I was there. A few moments later she led me into his office.

He seemed much older than I remembered, a small bent man with thick white hair and a leathery wrinkled face. He peered at me over steel-rimmed spectacles.

"Margaret Ashcroft . . . I heard you had returned to Harrowgate."

I couldn't be sure if his tone was disapproving or surprised. "I would have come sooner had I known my grandfather was ill," I said.

He nodded. "What is it you want to see me about, Miss Ashcroft?"

"Two things, actually. I tripped and twisted my ankle last night. It's much better but I thought you might take a look at it." I raised my foot and he motioned me to the examining table, taking my hand as I climbed up and he began to unwrap the bandage Emma had tied. The woman in white apron hovered with scissors and equipment.

I winced slightly as he probed at the bruised spots and moved my foot at various angles.

"No bones broken . . . a sprain. Should be all right in a day or two but I'll bind it up for you to make sure." The nurse handed him a roll of bandage and he began to wind it about my ankle. "What else did you want to see me about?" he said.

"I'm told you tended my grandfather before

he—when he was ill."

He snorted. "Saw him twice."

"You saw him at the beginning of his illness?"

He looked up at me, pushing the spectacles up on his nose where they had slid down. "Your grandfather had a heart attack. A young woman, who said she was engaged to your brother, sent for me when Franklin collapsed. I diagnosed the heart condition and left some medication for him."

He seemed reluctant to talk about the affair and I wondered why.

"Was it a serious attack?"

He glanced up briefly then resumed bandaging the foot. "I figured he'd recover in a month or so if he took it easy. Told the young lady that. Franklin was headstrong though, he wouldn't follow instructions. Next thing I knew I got a note to hurry right out—he'd taken a turn for the worse. Annie Newgate was tending him, but it was too late. He lapsed into a coma a few minutes after I got there." Doctor Foxx fastened a piece of tape to hold the bandage in place.

The nurse had said nothing but I felt her gaze on me. When I looked at her, she was scowling deeply and looked away.

"He had a second heart attack then?" I asked.

The doctor nodded.

"Does this happen?" I knew so little of medicine or illness.

He finished taping my foot and pushed his chair back. "The human heart is a delicate organ, Miss Ashcroft. Once it's been damaged it becomes a faulty mechanism and there's no telling what further problems will arise. Your grandfather was close to ninety years of age. He'd lived a full, robust life, and his heart finally gave out. If he didn't follow the medical prognosis I gave, there could be a dozen things to account for it. I suspect you've heard some of the gossip around the village. It's just that—gossip. People in these parts have never taken kindly to the people in the manor house, and stories are bound to come up."

His blue eyes seemed kindly behind the glasses all at once. "Your grandfather was lucid at the end, my dear. He mentioned your name and spoke of his letter to you."

"Letter? But I received no letter—"

"Perhaps he left it with someone?"

No one had come forward with a letter . . . I felt the nurse watching me and I was very uncomfortable under her stare. "Yes, that must be it. I'm sure it will turn up."

"Will you be staying on at Harrowgate?" the doctor asked.

I bit my lip. "Until my brother returns. I dislike leaving Juliette alone to handle matters." With a guilty start, I remembered Juliette's fragile condition. Quickly, I told the doctor about her and asked his advice.

He smiled. "If you're giving her one of

Annie's potions, Juliette is probably already on the road to recovery. See that she takes it every day. Fix her up in no time."

I was surprised to hear him praise the old woman's medical skills and relieved at the same time. Doctor Foxx noticed my expression and went on. "Old Annie's been healing folks in these parts long as anyone can remember. No sense denying she gets results, and people put a lot of faith in her. Your grandfather for one." He smiled. "So let Annie's magic elixir work for Juliette."

"She did look better this morning," I said.

The old man nodded and stood up, holding out a hand to help me down. "You look a bit tired yourself, young lady. Maybe you need a tonic."

I shook my head. "I haven't slept well—nothing more."

The nurse looked at me sharply, her eyes full of questions. "Tis said the ghosts of Harrowgate walk at night—"

"That will be enough of that, Mrs. Hanley," the doctor said. "Miss Ashcroft isn't interested in town gossip."

"But I am—really. I mean I'm not interested in gossip but I would like to know what is going on at Harrowgate."

"Going on? Why should anything be going on?" He sounded impatient and slightly annoyed.

"There have been several things happen that I have not been able to explain," I told him. "The village stories might help—"

"Nonsense. Imaginings of superstitious people. You'd do best not to involve yourself with them, young lady."

He was treating me like a child, and I felt annoyance. "Thank you, doctor. You may send the bill to Harrowgate." I took my leave, hobbling slightly on the bound foot.

I left the carriage where it was and walked toward Meyerin's store in the center of town. A soft breeze ruffled my skirts and the sun was warm. Several people nodded to me, but I sensed a reserve in the greetings. At Meyerin's, I purchased several bits of colored ribbon for Juliette's hair and some bright threads that might entice her to try some needlework. The shopkeeper wrapped them and handed them over without comment. I was sure he recognized me but he gave no sign of it. As I turned to leave I almost bumped into a woman entering. I recognized the postmistress, and greeted her warmly.

"Good morning, Mrs. Farrell."

She turned and stared past me, deliberately ignoring me. I felt my cheeks flame.

That much about Louthwick had not changed then. The townspeople still considered Harrowgate remote from their lives, a place of strangers who did not share the village life. I should not have expected different—

I limped toward the phaeton, eager to escape the cold indifference that surrounded me.

"Good morning, Miss Ashcroft."

Startled, I turned to see the constable regarding me curiously. "I'm sorry if I made you jump," he said.

"My mind was wandering, I'm sorry . . ."

"I saw you come out of the store and couldn't help noticing your foot. Had an accident, have you?" He looked genuinely concerned.

"It's only a minor sprain," I said. "Nothing serious."

"I'm glad of that." He fell in step with me, clasping his strong hands behind his back.

"People in the village are concerned about the body found in the woods," he said. "It's easy for them to connect such strange doings with the old stories about the manor house, Miss."

He had seen the encounter with Mrs. Farrell and was trying to soothe my wounded pride. I was grateful. "Yes, I suppose. Tell me, have you learned any more about the dead man?"

The constable shook his head. "Only that he'd asked questions about the manor house of several people. Just vanished then, and no one gave it a thought, what with him being a stranger. Figured he went back to wherever he came from."

A group of women emerged from the church across the street and one of them caught sight of me, stared, and hissed something to the others. I looked away, seeing that the constable had observed the exchange. His brow furrowed. "We're a small community," he said apologetically.

"Do the townspeople really think we're involved? Are they so willing to believe ill of Harrowgate?"

He took a deep breath and let it out slowly. "I'm afraid so, Miss. But you can hardly blame them."

"What in the world—"

"Maybe I shouldn't say it, Miss, but Harrowgate woods has had more than its share of strange deaths this past year."

I was shocked. "Deaths . . . you mean there's been another?"

He nodded. "It was put down as accidental, but people are beginning to wonder now."

I found it difficult to speak. "Who—?"

"I thought you knew, Miss. The newspapers—"

I shook my head. I'd read nothing of Louthwick or Harrowgate since I'd left four years ago. "This is the first I've heard of any death."

The constable shrugged thick shoulders. "It was several months ago. The body was found in the marsh. The gossipers say it was supernatural."

I found myself shivering, remembering my own terror at being alone in the dark marsh.

"The old stories about the curse have cropped up again."

"I've heard some of them," I said in a near whisper.

"Of course, I don't believe in ghosts." The constable smiled depreciatingly. "Nobody in his right mind would."

I looked at him, saying nothing. He was such a stolid looking man, the type to believe only what he could see and feel. I wondered what he would say if I told him of my experiences with ghostly apparitions. Instead I thanked him for his concern and assured him that I had no intentions of venturing into the woods. As for the tales of ghosts in the manor house, I said nothing. What could I say?

"You will be careful, Miss?"

That surprised me. "Do you think there is some danger at Harrowgate?" I asked.

He frowned. "I didn't say that, Miss. But if you see anyone about that doesn't belong, best you report it and let me have a look."

"You can be sure I will, Constable." I smiled as he helped me up into the phaeton and untied the reins.

Driving away, I wondered if I should have confided my suspicions that someone had been lurking in the woods that day . . . ?

Chapter Nine

As I rode past Meyerin's, a man emerged and stopped to stare at me. I had never seen him before, and the intensity of his gaze made me uncomfortable. It was almost as if he wanted to speak to me but hesitated for some reason known only to himself. He was tall, dressed in a riding coat that was more suitable to a hunt than for shopping in Louthwick. I turned as our eyes met, and I urged the horse to speed its pace. Without turning, I was sure the man was watching until I was out of sight around the bend of the road, past the schoolhouse where a bell pealed sharply and children spilled from the doorway into the yard.

The pleasure of the earlier drive had vanished, and I was depressed and eager to get home. Ever since my arrival at Harrowgate, I had been filled with a sense of foreboding, a resurrection of the memories of my unhappiness here. As soon as Juliette was well enough to travel, I would suggest we return to London—

I brought my thoughts up short. I had no

place to go in London! I had run away from my job and my past as well as my broken romance with Edward Law. I had told Mrs. Nottingham, my landlady, that I would not be back. She would have let my rooms by now. It might take me awhile to find another position and be able to support myself. I had little choice but to stay on at Harrowgate until Charles returned and considered my plight.

I made a mental note to ask Wiley Temple if my grandfather had left me any bequest. Even a few hundred pounds would see me through until I found another job and rebuilt my life.

The sky was no longer clear; flat grey wisps were beginning to roll into storm clouds, darkening the day. The wind had picked up and I hugged my coat around me as the horse sensed the storm and hastened toward home. How sharp the English country weather was, and how unpredictable.

I saw the woods ahead, and the road began to climb in a gradual slope. It was not far to Harrowgate, and my chances of beating the storm were good. I had no desire to be on the twisting road when the rain began. The way the wind was blowing, I would be drenched in the open carriage. A bolt of lightning crashed through the trees ahead and thunder rolled.

The horse shied, rearing on its hind legs and neighing loudly, head thrashing and feet stomping. I grabbed the reins and tried to control him, but he was too frightened. He bolted, bouncing the carriage along and almost knocking me from the seat with the suddenness of the motion. I clutched the rail and held on.

The phaeton swerved wildly behind the racing animal. I had lost the reins, and it was all I could do to keep my seat. My hat flew from my head, the ribbons catching about my throat like clawing fingers. The carriage groaned and creaked as though it would split. It skittered from side to side, once nearly overturning. I shrieked soundlessly into the wind.

I felt the sudden lurch as the carriage swerved off the road. A wheel struck a stone—and the crunch of splintering wood cracked sharply. My hands wrenched from the rail and I was pitched from the carriage. Dark tree branches seemed to reach, clawing and grabbing, as I was flung to the earth. Briars caught at my coat and face as I landed heavily on a soft carpet of leaves.

I lay stunned, the air knocked out of me and my head ringing with the force of my landing. I was staring up at the grey sky— seen through the thick tangle of evergreens vaulted above me.

I remained still until the fiery pain in my chest eased and I could breathe again. I was aware of the horse still running, dragging the broken phaeton along behind him in his terror. I turned my head in time to see him vanish beyond a bend in the road.

I sat up, moving my limbs gingerly and brushing damp leaves and bits of grass from my clothing. When I tried to stand, I was dizzy and had to lean against a tree to steady myself. The taped ankle shot pains up to my knee when I put weight on my foot.

I sighed, staring at the ribbon of road that wound through the woods. It was a long climb by foot to the house, but I had no choice, unless I wanted to wait until the horse reached home and hope that someone would come to investigate. Thunder rumbled overhead, settling the matter. I hobbled out to the road and began to walk.

I had gone only a few yards when I heard the noise of a vehicle behind me. I turned, moving to the side of the road and out of the way. Had someone else from Harrowgate gone into the village?

A small four wheeled cart pulled by a grey came into sight and the driver reined in the horse at once. I recognized the man I'd seen come out of Meyerin's shop—the man who stared at me. He was regarding me now with brooding eyes.

He climbed down from the cart. "Are you all right, Miss Ashcroft?"

"Yes—I think so. My horse bolted and the carriage hit a stone—" I glanced helplessly along the road where the horse had disappeared.

"Here, let me help you. I'll drive you to the house." He took my arm and propelled me to the cart, helping me up, then taking his place beside me. The first spatters of rain struck my face as he snapped the reins and the grey stepped into motion. I was not accustomed to accepting rides from strangers but again, I had no choice. The cart creaked and moved forward.

After several moments, I found him glancing at me again. I felt much ill at ease, wondering who he was and how he knew my name.

"I saw you in the village," I said.

He nodded and said nothing.

"This road leads to Harrowgate. Were you on your way there?"

He glanced sidelong at me, then said, "No."

He offered no further explanation, and I felt as though I'd been rebuked for asking questions that were none of my concern. But if he had not been on his way to the manor house, had he been following me?

I stared straight ahead until we came over the crest of a small rise and onto the tree-bordered drive leading to the house. The rain was still spattering down but the full fury of the storm had not broken, although the sky was ominous and thunder rumbled.

He drew up in front of the house and watched me climb down. "Thank you, Mr.—"

He stared, then said, "Paul Scofield. I've leased the cottage at the far side of the hill, beyond the woods." He tipped his hat and snapped the reins on the mare's flank. Without a backward glance, he turned the cart and went off down the drive.

How incredibly rude—yet he had saved me from a drenching and a very long walk. The rain was coming down in a burst now, and I scurried for the door and let myself in quickly.

"Good heavens! What in the world happened to you, Margaret?" Wiley had just emerged from the library and was gaping at my smudged and rumpled clothes. He came forward solicitously as I untied my bonnet strings and ran my hand over my hair. I knew I must look a sight.

I tried to smile. "The horse bolted and threw me out of the wagon. I'm afraid the phaeton is badly damaged—"

"Never mind the carriage," he said anxiously, "are you hurt?"

"No, I'm quite all right."

"How did you get home?"

"A man in a cart stopped for me and was kind enough to bring me to the door. A Mr. Scofield. He says he's leased the house at the other end of the woods." I dimly recalled a cottage at the edge of the road beyond the fork that circled the hill. I could not remember who owned it or who had ever lived there, if anyone.

Wiley looked startled. "The Rutherford cottage? Then he must be the man who discovered the body in the woods—Did the constable say he was an artist?"

I paled. I had not made the connection. Unnerved, I stammered, "I—I don't know." I felt a dreadful certainty that Paul Scofield had been following me—just as he had been watching me in the woods yesterday. I shivered.

Wiley took my arm solicitously and gazed at me. "Here now, you're chilled."

"It's nothing." I was aware of my disheveled appearance and Wiley's intimate gaze. I did not want to tell him my fears about Paul Scofield and give him further cause to worry.

"Upstairs with you," he said firmly but not unkindly. "Your clothes are damp and I won't have you falling ill."

With a grateful smile, I nodded and started up the stairs. On the fourth step, I turned guiltily to find him watching me. "The horse—please ask Lionel to see if it found its way home—"

"I'll take care of it." He waved me on, smiling but his eyes mirroring concern.

I blushed and hurried up to my room. To my surprise, I found myself humming softly as I changed my dress and spread my cloak over a chair to dry.

Warm and in dry clothes, I took the ribbons and thread to Juliette's room, only to find her asleep. I laid the things on the table and left.

In the kitchen, Mrs. Dobbs fixed me a cup of soup and some tea. I carried them to the library where I touched a match to the fire that was laid, then curled up in the big leather armchair before it. The soup and tea warmed me and I settled down to read and rest my ankle. I found myself drowsing over the pages and it was difficult to keep my attention on the book, and I soon set it aside. The morning's adventures had tired me more than I'd thought; the rain pounding against the window was a monotonous sound that half lulled me to sleep. I relaxed and let my mind drift. The memory of the horse taking fright and the accident that followed returned, and I shivered. The woods had seemed so dark then, and I was sure that the spot where the accident had happened was the same one where I'd seen the ghostly figure of the old man the night of my arrival. The woods. . . .

Was there truth in the village stories? The woods seemed a place of evil, especially with the rank treacherous swamp and the thick clawing growth at the end where the ground was lower. From it had grown the legend of Harrowgate, based on the long-ago death of Elizabeth Ashcroft. It had claimed two more lives, according to the constable.

I shook off my lethargy and gazed about the room. Tall, narrow leaded glass windows alternated with mahogany bookcases. There were many large portraits of family members, the Ashcrofts of bygone years. I rose from the chair and went to inspect them more closely. I recognized a few, remembering names from my childhood. A young soldier who had died in the Napoleonic Wars . . . a haughty woman with a hairstyle of two hundred years past—my grandfather's great-great grandmother, I thought. . . .

I walked about the room, glancing at pictures and the tiny brass nameplates. On the third wall, the portraits were more recent . . . my father, young and with a hint of devilment in his eyes as though he were planning some trick on the artist . . . and my mother as a young woman, pretty and shy looking, in a white muslin sprigged with pink roses. The plaque under it said Ellen Barnes Ashcroft. Mother had been only eighteen when she married Trevor Ashcroft, the same year the portrait was painted, I suspected. The artist had caught the essence of her personality that I had heard others speak of but so dimly recalled myself.

I sighed and moved to the portrait of my grandfather and studied it. It was done with him sitting at the great desk which still stood in the center of this very room. He looked much as I remember him, stern and rigid, his lips tight and his jaw set. His sparse white hair was combed neatly over his pate and his eyes glinted with cold light.

"Such a change," a voice said close behind me.

I started, unaware that anyone had entered the room, and found Becky regarding the portrait solemnly.

"A change?" I asked.

The girl nodded. "He looked so different those last months, not at all like the picture."

"In what way?"

She frowned, still staring at the portrait. "Thinner, of course; he lost a lot of weight so he was hardly more than skin and bones. And his eyes so wild-like! Looked a regular fright sometimes, but no one dared say anything. His temper—" She broke off, remembering to whom she was talking.

"I understand," I said, smiling. "His temper was never sweet even when he was not ill."

She nodded and ventured a small smile. "When he'd take a notion to wander about, no one could stop him. Miss Juliette was beside herself, she was."

"Wander about? You mean he wasn't bed-ridden all the time?"

"Oh no, Miss. He was up and about for several weeks before he was took bad again." She shook her head. "Wandering about in that long nightshirt and with his hair and beard all every which way—enough to scare you out of your wits if you came upon him unexpected!"

I glanced at the portrait, then back at Becky. "His hair and beard?"

She nodded. "Let them grow all straggly and long. . . ."

The apparition in the road! She was giving me a description of Franklin Ashcroft!

"Oh dear . . . I almost forgot . . . Miss Juliette is awake and asking for you, Miss."

"Thank you, I'll go right up."

The girl bobbed and left as I took a final look at my grandfather's portrait. I had not seen the features of the figure on the road but it *could* have been him. Had he been warning me of some danger? Danger here at Harrowgate?

I hurried upstairs and found Juliette sitting up in bed, smiling as she brushed her long dark hair. She looked relaxed and rested and her eyes sparkled.

"You brought me ribbons—how thoughtful!"

I crossed to the bed and took the brush from her hand and began to stroke her hair. "I had thought the sun would be out all day and we might sit in the garden, but the weather is being capricious again."

"I hate the rain," she said, shuddering slightly, then smiling. "But it's not so bad now that you are here. I'm glad you've come, Margaret. It's a miracle how much better I feel all at once."

"You should have written me sooner, dear. It was too much for you to take care of grandfather by yourself."

She turned to look at me. "I didn't, really—Annie did most of the nursing. Grandfather liked to have me near, that's all."

"But—" The Mundys had said Juliette wore herself out caring for the old man.

She seemed eager to talk. "I'd never nursed anyone and hardly knew what to do. I was so frightened when I found him that day—"

"Don't talk about it if it upsets you, Juliette."

She shook her head. "No, I want to tell you. He was your grandfather and you've all been so good to me. . . ." She smiled, touching my hand as I set aside the brush and began tying a yellow ribbon in her hair.

When I finished, she lay back. "He'd been upset for several weeks, withdrawn. He seemed to be brooding over something, you know, worried, but he didn't say what it was. He took to getting up during the night and wandering about the house as if he were looking for something. I tried to find out what was troubling him but he'd shake his head and tell me not to worry about it, that he'd get to the bottom of the matter and then there would be some pleasant surprises in store for a lot of people."

"What kind of pleasant surprises?"

"He wouldn't say. He acted mysterious and didn't want to talk about it, so I didn't pry."

She went on with her story: Often at night she heard tapping from various parts of the house and she'd find the old man banging walls, moving furniture. One night, something woke her, she wasn't sure what, and when she looked for him she found him crumpled in a heap in the upper hall. She called the Mundys to help her get him to bed and sent for the doctor immediately. Dr. Foxx diagnosed a heart attack, telling them to keep him quiet and give him the medicine he left. The old man seemed dazed when he came to, and weak from his ordeal. He said little and seemed to watch the others warily.

"He was so remote, almost as if he didn't know me," Juliette said. "Yet the doctor had said he would be all right, and I thought the strangeness would pass."

He regained his strength and the next thing she knew, he was wandering about again. Nothing she could do would convince him he had to stay in bed. He'd be docile and silent all day, and as soon as the household was abed, he'd resume his nocturnal prowling and tapping.

Juliette sighed and her eyes clouded. "He began wandering about the grounds and in the old east wing. Oh, Margaret, I was so frightened but I couldn't stop him." She was close to tears, and I put my arms around her.

"There now, you did all you could. Grandfather was very stubborn and if he made up his mind to do something, no one would change it."

She smiled weakly. "Yes, I know you're right. Charles warned me of that when he brought me here."

She continued her story. One morning, she woke to find his bed empty. With the Mundys and Becky, she combed the house without success. Lionel found the old man in the east wing. He'd collapsed with another attack and laid in the chill all night. Annie came at once

120

but there was little she could do. Juliette summoned the doctor, hoping for some miracle, but it was too late. The old man's weakened condition and the second heart attack were too much, and he died two days later.

Juliette sighed and brushed away a tear. "He knew he was dying and it seemed to make him angry. I think because he had not accomplished whatever it was he was trying to do those last weeks when he roamed about the house searching. . . ."

"Didn't he tell you what he'd been up to? A deathbed confession or explanation?"

"No. Several times I thought he was about to but he was distracted before he did. He fell asleep easily, sometimes in mid-sentence."

I patted her hand. "He was a very old man, Juliette, and he lived a full life. I don't think he'd want you to grieve."

"Yes, I suppose you're right." She smiled. "It was you he spoke of in his final moments, Margaret."

The doctor had said much the same thing, and again I was surprised. I had not been close to my grandfather and I believed he had cared little for me. "What did he say?"

She frowned, trying to remember. "Something about a letter he'd written you—"

The letter . . . did it exist or was it a figment of an old man's wandering mind? I had never received a letter of any kind from him, I was sure. I put aside the thoughts and turned the conversation to more cheerful subjects, telling Juliette bits of gossip and news from London, elaborating on my life there and making it sound frivolous and gay. I carefully avoided all mention of Edward and my shattered romance.

The afternoon passed quickly; by dinner time Juliette looked tired but more cheerful than I'd seen her, and I was convinced that she would be well soon. I went to my room to freshen up, then descended to the dining room.

Dinner was a silent affair, with Becky looking strangely red-eyed and tense as she served, throwing hostile glances at Emma Mundy each time she passed. What had happened between them? I was even more curious that Wiley did not offer me more than a casual smile.

With the bread pudding dessert, I brought up the subject of the letter. Three faces turned to me.

"Both the doctor and Juliette say my grandfather spoke of a letter he wrote me. Did he have any secret places for keeping such things?" I asked.

Lionel scowled. "None—I'm sure of it. I would have known."

"It's more than likely that he never wrote the letter at all. It was one of his failings these past years—planning things he never got around to. He talked a good deal and I think he sometimes convinced himself he'd already done them."

I was reluctant to believe that, but I did not argue. I had not seen my grandfather for four years and many changes had occurred it seemed.

"Did he say what was in the letter?" Wiley asked. "Perhaps it was nothing more than a restatement of his will."

"I don't know," I said honestly. His remark reminded me of another question I'd been meaning to ask. "What of my grandfather's will, Wiley? Am I mentioned in it, perhaps some small bequest?"

He looked at me sharply. "Of course you are, my dear. How remiss of me not to have told you. Your grandfather left you several hundred pounds outright. The house and properties go to your brother, of course, passing to you only in the event of his death without heirs."

I had little interest in owning Harrowgate; the bequest of cash would be enough to let me establish a new life and build my own future away from here. Harrowgate held nothing but sad memories for me.

Wiley was speaking again. "I shall take care of the details immediately. I plan to return to London tomorrow for several days and I shall arrange everything."

"Thank you." I hid my disappointment that he was leaving.

It was later in my room that I realized the subject of the letter had not been resolved. I was startled by a rap at my door, and even more surprised to find Becky standing there when I opened it. Dusk had fallen and I had thought her already on her way home.

"Please, Miss, I had to tell you I didn't do it—no matter wot she says!"

I drew her into the room, so terrified did she seem, glancing over her shoulder repeatedly to make sure no one overheard. "Do what, Becky?"

She was distraught, wringing her hands and picking at the dark shawl she'd thrown over her shoulders. She was obviously finished with her work for the day and ready to leave.

"I didn't steal it. I wouldn't do a thing like that. I'm an honest girl—"

"Of course you are, Becky. Please, calm down and tell me what it is."

She took a deep breath and stood straight. "Mis Mundy accused me of taking that lovely shawl, the one from your closet—you asked me about it yesterday. But I didn't Miss Margaret, I swear I didn't!"

"I believe you, Becky. Why would Mrs. Mundy say such a thing?"

The girl's eyes were wide. "She claims she found it on the floor down at the end of the hall. Said I must have dropped it when someone came upstairs unexpected. I told her it was yours, that I'd seen it in your closet."

"But it isn't mine," I said. "And you can't have stolen something that wasn't mine in the first place, now could you?"

She nodded and looked relieved. "Still, it

ain't right her accusing me that way. I never touched the shawl at all. I don't know how it got there, honestly."

"Let's not say anymore about it, all right? I'm sure there's an explanation. I'll talk to Mrs. Mundy myself if it will make you feel better."

"Oh thank you, Miss. I don't like being thought a thief." She glanced at the window and gasped. "I must be off, it'll be dark soon—" She turned and hurried out.

I watched her out of sight down the stairs, wondering the while why Emma Mundy had made such a fuss about a shawl. Was she deliberately trying to antagonize the girl? Puzzled, I walked to the wardrobe and saw that the green shawl was once again on the shelf. I lifted it down and carried it to the mirror, draping the filmy lace over my shoulders and staring at my image in the glass. It was like a feathery cobweb on the pink calico I wore, casting a faint glow that seemed to light my face. I turned the glass, letting it catch the reflection of the portrait of Elizabeth beside my own. We looked like twin images in the glass, and I smiled.

I thought the girl in the picture smiled also.

Chapter Ten

I fell asleep quickly, with the sound of the rain whispering against the windows. It had slackened somewhat during the evening, settling to a soaking drizzle.

When I woke, the room was dark and an eerie stillness filled it. I strained to listen for the pattering but heard nothing. Yet there was no light, no moon to ease the hard shadows. I turned and drew the covers about me, unwilling to wake completely yet aware that I had been disturbed by something. It was as though someone were watching me—

I opened my eyes and glanced about the room. Under the portrait of Elizabeth Ashcroft, two people stood—no, not persons—apparitions. I recognized Elizabeth and a young man.

He was smiling, looking down at Elizabeth with tenderness and love, tilting her chin so he could cover her lips with his. Elizabeth responded eagerly, throwing herself into his arms and hugging herself to him.

I felt embarrassed at witnessing such intimacy. I was seeing Elizabeth, the bride, and her young groom, Harland Beaumont. Was this their bedchamber?

The couple kissed again; laughing, the young man swept the girl off her feet, carrying her in his arms toward the bed. So real was the vision, I found myself scrambling, ready to dart from the bed as they approached.

But they vanished then, fading as though some inner light had been extinguished, and I was alone in the room. I sat staring about. I was witnessing the happiness of the young couple as they began their life together, before the tragedy of the missing jewels and death.

I could not understand why these strange visions returned to me. Was it because I was in *this* room—the bridal chamber of Elizabeth Ashcroft? Was Elizabeth trying to tell me something?

I had never been visited by ghosts before in my life, and the notion that they might impart messages to me was laughable. Still, the figure in the road had warned me away from Harrowgate. I was convinced now that the figure had been Grandfather Franklin. Becky's description had been too accurate for doubt.

I became aware of a sound that had been on the edge of my consciousness for several minutes. A tapping noise. I cocked my head to listen but it was so faint I could not determine its source. I tried to dismiss it as I lay down and closed my eyes determinedly, but it was no use. I had to know where it was coming from. Sighing, I got up and slipped into my robe. Like Elizabeth Ashcroft's ghost, I seemed destined to wander the halls of Harrowgate every night!

The sound was less distinct in the hall, so I turned back to the window and drew open the drapes. The light across the yard caught my eye instantly, and I raised the sash to listen. A hammering sound was coming from the east wing, from the direction of the light I could see blinking as something—or someone—passed in front of it.

The east wing was closed, had been as long as I could remember. Lionel Mundy said it was unused, and according to Becky, the east wing was haunted. Ghosts hammering by lamplight?

I knew I should return to bed and leave my quest until daylight, but I'd already had enough implications that I suffered from delusions. If no one wanted to discuss the strange nighttime occurrences that seemed to abound at Harrowgate, I would find out for myself. More than anything, I wanted to prove myself to Wiley, I realized.

I lighted the lamp and took the precaution of dropping several matches into my robe pocket before I let myself out of the room. The lamp was turned low, and I shielded its pale glow with my hand as I moved along the dark hall. The house was silent, with no moonlight at the windows to relieve the blackness. The carpet muffled the sound of my footsteps as I passed the closed doors along the passage.

The east wing opened off the long hall that ran from front to back of the house. I had done no more than glance this way, but I knew the wide doors that had once stood open between the two sections of the house would be closed and locked. But there was a key. It hung where it always had near the top of the lintel; I found it without trouble and inserted it in the lock. The bolt clicked back and I drew the door open, slipping inside.

I lifted the lamp and peered about the musty hall. Cobwebs fluttered as I passed and patterns of dust on the parquet floor had not been disturbed for a long time. Whoever was using the east wing had not come this way.

Ghosts do not leave footprints . . .

Stop it! I told myself. But even as I did, I saw the two figures ahead of me, gliding soundlessly along the musty hall. One was the young man I'd seen with Elizabeth in the bed-chamber; the other was older by a few years, dark haired, with a full mustache and wearing a dark frock coat, somewhat the worse for wear, and showing spots of grime along the sleeves and a torn place at one of the pockets. His trousers were dusty and his shoes caked with mud as though he had walked a long way. It was obvious that they were arguing, although not a sound broke the eerie silence of the hall.

I became aware then of what sounded like

the music of a stringed orchestra at a great distance . . . somewhere below me. The great ballroom had once occupied the lower floor of the east wing.

The figures moved toward the closed doors of the upper hall. They were both furious, and the phantom anger seemed to fill the hall. The man turned suddenly and grabbed Harland by the coat. Harland swung out at him, and they grappled, their shadowy figures merging as the blows fell silently. The scene was even more frightening for the absence of sound, and I pressed against the wall in terror. Elizabeth's bridegroom reeled as the other struck him; he hit the wall and crumpled to the floor. The dark man in the frock coat stood over him a moment, then reached into his pocket.

For a moment I stared, unable to believe my eyes or senses. The man was holding a brass-hilted dagger, bending over Harland and menacing him with the tip of the weapon at his throat. A tiny drop of blood gathered above the frilly collar of Harland's ball costume and his eyes widened with terror. The man looming over him laughed and drew back, wiping the blade on his sleeve and slipping the dagger back into his pocket as he strode away. I watched until he vanished into the shadows at the end of the hall. When I looked back, Harland had also vanished and I was alone.

I was still leaning against the wall, my

heart throbbing and my breath coming in painful gasps as though I had been running hard. I had witnessed a murderous anger—and a threat of possible further violence between the two men. I felt cold and very sad. . . .

The music ceased as I came back to the present with a jolt. I was once more aware of the tapping sound that had lured me here. It was louder now, coming from somewhere ahead of me, behind one of the closed doors of the upper hall. The few times I had been in this portion of the house had not left a clear memory of its layout, and I tried to orient myself. From my room, the light I'd seen would be at the far end of the wing, on this level. . . .

I heard a small scurrying sound and closed my mind to the thought of mice or other creatures in the shadows around me. My heart was still pounding and my throat was dry. I was beginning to regret my curiosity.

I glimpsed the light then, a faint line at the bottom of a door. I tiptoed toward it, knees shaking and pulse throbbing. The knob turned silently under my hand and the door swung inward with a creak. The light inside went out, plunging the room into darkness. I held my breath, listening. . . .

"Who's there?" I called, my voice wavering. I hoped I sounded more brave than I felt. I was ten kinds of fool to venture here alone! Suppose the stranger I'd seen lingering about the drive and entering this wing was a thief—or a murderer?! The body in the woods—

I heard a whisper of sound and poked the lamp into the room. Huge shadows fell in shimmering blotches, casting images upon the wall that seemed to close in on me.

"Who's there?" I demanded, but the words came out as barely a whisper. The silence was listening . . . waiting. . . .

There was a swirl of motion in a corner, a white misty fog rose from the floor and took shape—the shape of a man! My heart raced and I could scarcely breathe. The figure seemed to stare right at me, waving its arms and urging me back. . . . It was the same figure I'd seen in the road. Grandfather Franklin!

In numb terror, I backed out, my hand groping the door jamb as my eyes were riveted on the ghostly figure that advanced on me.

A sudden gust of air made the lamp sputter, and I uttered another frightened cry as the lamp flickered and went out. I fumbled in my pocket for a match, terrified of the darkness and even more terrified of what lurked in it. I tried to grope my way along the corridor, retracing my steps to the door through which I'd come, but I stumbled and almost dropped the lamp. Shaking with fright, I leaned against the wall and took deep breaths until my hand was steady enough to strike a match. There was no other sound near me, no hint of a presence other than my own.

The match flared and I bent quickly to set down the lamp and remove the chimney. The hot glass burned my fingers and I cried out with pain. By the flare of the match, I tried to locate the hall I'd come through. Crouching there, I saw the light glint on two beady eyes only a few feet away. I smothered a scream and a fat creature darted into the darkness as the match burned out and I was once more plunged into darkness.

I pulled myself up, hand on the wall to guide me, and moved as quickly as I dared. Did I hear footsteps behind me or was it my imagination . . . ?

I was sobbing now, shivering and rushing headlong through the passageway toward the main wing. The door I had unlocked stood open, making a subtle difference in the darkness so I was able to see my way. I pulled the door shut but didn't pause to lock it, fleeing immediately to my own room. I bolted myself in and stood gasping in near panic. With shaking hands, I found another lamp and lighted it, staring at myself in the mirror and shocked by the wide-eyed image, hair awry, that stared back at me! If I hadn't been so frightened, I might have laughed.

This time there was no doubt in my mind—it had been Grandfather Franklin, and he had been warning me away from whatever evil lay within that room.

What had it been?

For a long time I stared from the window and tried to catch a glint of light in the east wing but seeing nothing but the unrelieved blackness of the night. I was wide awake, too aware that what had happened could not possibly have been a dream. I paced the room but could not bring myself to venture into the hall again. After a very long time I climbed back into bed and fell into a troubled sleep.

All traces of the storm were gone when I woke. I could tell by the patterns along the drive that the sun was high, the morning almost gone. Despite the hours of sleep, I did not feel rested.

Downstairs, Mrs. Dobbs informed me that Wiley Temple had left for London and that Lionel and Emma had driven him to the village to the station in order that they might do some shopping also. I felt strangely relieved to know that Juliette and I were alone in the house except for the servants.

After breakfast, I went up to Juliette's room and with Becky's help, got her out of bed and downstairs. We sat in two lawn chairs in the garden, Juliette with a warm afghan wrapped about her even though the day was mild. I was determined to be cheerful, and Juliette was soon laughing happily and chattering about her girlhood, her romance with Charles, their plans for the future. I was surprised to hear that she'd been looking forward to living at Harrowgate, and that Charles had spoken eagerly of returning.

I had imagined Charles felt much as I did about Harrowgate, and I would have thought him reluctant to even return. I might do well to re-examine my own thoughts and discover if my dislike for the old manor house was based on childish judgments. I had been a shy, lonely child . . . I might have seen the world around me through a haze. . . .

Juliette brought up the subject of Charles' absence and a tiny worried frown appeared again between her brows. "It isn't like him not to write. . . ."

"Please, dear, don't worry yourself. If it will make you feel better, I'll start inquiries."

She looked at me hopefully. "Would you? There must be some way to determine if he's left Cape Town."

"Do you know which vessel he planned to sail on?"

She shook her head. "Are there that many from South Africa?"

I had to confess that I didn't know. Perhaps Wiley Temple could advise me. I would ask him as soon as he returned.

"Have you written to Charles lately?"

"Oh yes, I write almost every day. Mrs. Mundy takes the letters to the village." She sighed and stared off at the sun glistening on the hills. A songbird trilled a melody, and for a moment the world seemed suspended in peace. My gaze fell on the edge of the woods, and I saw a flash of color and movement. My eye caught it again, and I glimpsed the figure of a man as he stepped quickly behind a tree.

I stared, trying to discern more but failing. It was as if the man had been aware of my glance and tried to avoid being seen. Jonathon Newgate? Somehow my mind rejected the thought. The figure had been shorter, less powerful . . . yet I was sure it was familiar.

For an instant, the man stepped into view again, seeming to look directly at me. Then he was gone. The thicket rustled as though a breeze had passed, then was still.

"What is it, Margaret?" Juliette was watching me with a puzzled look, glancing over her shoulder in the direction of my stare.

I brought myself up abruptly. "Nothing, a bird darting among the branches. I think you've had enough fresh air for one day. Come, let's go inside."

I threw aside the cover and took her arm as she got to her feet. Very slowly, we started toward the house as Becky came running to help. She babbled about how well Juliette was doing, keeping up a line of chatter until we were indoors, relieving me of the necessity to speak.

It gave me a few minutes to pull myself together, for I now recognized the figure near the woods. Memories had meshed and I was sure the watchful figure staring up at us was the man who'd come along so opportunely after the carriage mishap . . . the stranger who was staying at the cottage across the woods. What was Paul Scofield doing at Harrowgate . . . ?

Chapter Eleven

I puzzled over the strange actions of Paul Scofield throughout lunch, dining alone in the huge dining room since the Mundys had not yet returned. Twice I had discovered him on Harrowgate property, and neither time had he come to the house. I considered calling the constable and asking him to investigate, but Scofield hadn't actually *done* anything. Matter of fact, he had helped me from a desperate plight.

I asked Mrs. Dobbs the location of the Rutherford cottage, then set out for the stables. They were no longer magnificent as they had once been; grandfather had kept a dozen fine horses, and a full-time stableboy to tend them. There were only two animals now. I avoided the chestnut who had shied at thunder and spilled me from the phaeton, selecting instead the mare who looked like she might be accustomed to riders. It had been a long time since I'd saddled a horse but I managed and was soon riding the animal down the slope of the meadow, following a faint trail that circled the hill above the woods and wound along a stream that flowed into the marsh. I had no desire to enter the woods, and Mrs. Dobbs had assured me that this path would take me out to the road and the Rutherford cottage.

The afternoon was brisk and pleasant, with a vast blue sky and only a few white clouds for trimming. The sun was warm and the mare walked sedately and seemed to know the path; I was content to let her pick her own way for the most part as I viewed the scenery trying to recapture the feeling of beauty Harrowgate had once held for me.

The horse was a beautiful black animal, graceful and spirited. Once we had gained the bridle path along the stream, she seemed eager to run and I let her have her head. She galloped briskly, and I felt the wind at my hair, fanning it out behind me since I had not pinned it nor worn a cap. Much of the tension of the past days vanished, and I felt exhilarated. The mare veered from the path and took a trail that wound through the sundappled trees bordering the meadow. She slowed finally when we reached the top of a rise and the hill fell away sharply to a ravine at the other side. The scene was magnificent; the entire valley lay below, the village like a toy town in the distance, the near hills green with spring except where the soil had been plowed and planted. I saw the Rutherford cottage nestled against the base of the hill near the fork in the road.

Gently I nudged the horse on the down slope, coaxing her along the narrow trail that led to the valley floor. The black seemed nervous and picked her way gingerly. Perhaps it was a mistake . . . the trail was quite steep all at once and I had not ridden for years . . . I clutched the reins and spoke gently to the horse.

"Steady, girl . . . easy now . . ."

The shot was loud, cracking so close I imagined I heard the bullet dig into a nearby tree. Then there was time to think of nothing—the horse threw up her head, rearing and slipping down the steep grade, digging in and trying to brace herself as we plummeted down the hill. I screamed as the brush and trees rushed toward me, branches clawing at my clothes, vines and twigs grasping at my face.

Then I was falling, sliding and scrambling as the horse whinnied in terror and rolled free. I clawed with both hands, grabbing at anything that might break my fall. The mare had come to a halt on a narrow fold of ground that was wide enough to stand on, and was trembling and shaking, looking up at me with terrified eyes.

I grabbed a sapling and the sharp bark cut at my palm, slipping through my grasp and sending me plummeting again. I bounced over several rocks and felt the edges cut my flesh. Once my head came in contact with something very hard and I was momentarily stunned. I slid past the ledge, unable to reach out and pull myself onto it. With dizzying speed, the bottom of the ravine raced toward me. I was only half conscious as I felt the hard pressure on my arm and realized something had stopped my descent.

I lay sobbing, unable to believe that I had been saved. My head hurt and my hands felt as though they had been burned raw. I moaned and opened my eyes.

I found myself staring up into Paul Scofield's face. I couldn't have been more surprised!

"Are you all right?" he said.

"I—I think so—"

"You little fool," he said, "you might have been killed!"

With effort, I raised my head and let him help me to a sitting position. His words angered me but I could find no retort. "Thank you for saving me." I was very sincere.

He grunted, helping me up as I stumbled to my feet and tried to brush my riding dress.

"What are you doing here?"

"Obviously I was out riding. I didn't realize the hill was so steep, and when the horse was frightened by the shot—" I looked at him, noting for the first time that he carried no gun. Who then . . . ?

He scowled. "Some poacher, no doubt. People aren't used to riders being about." He glanced around, staring at the trees on the crest of the hill for a long time before he turned away. "I suggest you ride back by the road—unless you want me to take you in the cart."

I shook my head, looking at the mare who had found an easy descent and was now placidly cropping grass at the foot of the hill. "I can ride back. Thank you again for saving me from a nasty fall."

He nodded but did not let go of my arm as he led me down the hill and to the horse. I saw then his artist's easel and supplies set up several yards away. He had been painting a landscape, and the scattered brushes gave mute testimony to his quick action when he saw my fall.

"If you would like a cup of tea, my cottage is just beyond the bend," he said.

I hesitated, then agreed. "I would appreciate it." After all, I had come to see him or at least to find out more about him. My plan had been half formed at best, but now he was inviting me to the cottage. I would never have a better chance to learn more about him.

He collected his easel and canvas, tucking the paint box under his arm. Catching the mare's reins and leading her behind us, we walked across the meadow. The cottage was tiny, scarcely bigger than Annie's but set in the bright sunlight of the meadow instead of a woodsy clearing. The yard had been well kept, with a freshly painted fence and a bed of tulips in bloom near the doorway. I wondered how long Paul Scofield had been living here.

He moved about the tiny kitchen, putting a kettle on to boil and setting out the teapot and cups. He said nothing as he prepared the tea and waited for it to steep. I began to think he planned not to speak to me at all, and I could think of no remark that would not make me sound foolish. I couldn't come right out and ask him to explain his presence near Harrowgate.

He poured the tea, watching me as he did so. "What made you choose that ridge for your ride?" he asked finally.

"I don't know—chance, I guess. I had no idea it might be dangerous."

"You seem to encounter a lot of dangerous situations, young lady."

"Not of my choosing, I assure you!" I felt as though he were scolding me, and I found myself bristling. Annoyed, I went on. "You manage to turn up in unexpected places when I get in trouble, Mr. Scofield, almost as though—" I flushed when he looked at me sharply. I *was* grateful, but his attitude piqued me. Despite my annoyance, I felt curiously safe with him. I sipped the tea and looked about the cottage. He kept it neat, with none of the clutter Charles had seemed to accumulate. He'd set the easel and paints on a rack near the door; several canvases were propped against the wall nearby; a pipe lay in an ashtray on the small table near the window. Otherwise the room was pin-neat, swept and dusted and cheerful. The windowpanes sparkled in the sunshine.

"How long have you lived here?" I asked him.

"A few weeks," he said. "I came down from London last month."

"The weather's been cold—for painting, I mean."

He smiled at my obvious prying. He seemed not to mind. "I've worked indoors. The light is good here. Today was one of the first outdoor sessions I've tried."

"Lucky for me."

He smiled and glanced over his shoulder at me as he lifted the tea cosy and refilled our cups. "Something's going on at Harrowgate, you know . . ."

"What?"

He turned back with the cups and stood looking down at me. "I wish I knew, but I think you may be in danger."

"I—why do you say such a thing?"

He resumed his seat without taking his eyes from me. "Isn't it obvious? The accident with the wagon, the fall from the horse—"

I shook my head impatiently. "But that's it—they were accidents! I was alone both times!"

"And both times you had a horse you knew little about. . . . Did you know that either of them would bolt at loud noises?"

Surprised, I shook my head. I couldn't deny what he was saying—the wagon incident had occurred because of thunder and my fall had come about because of a shot by an unseen hunter. Paul Scofield was saying they were deliberate attempts to harm me.

"Why would anyone want to harm me?" I had been frightened but I'd never considered any deliberate scheming behind the incidents.

He picked up his pipe and tamped tobacco into the bowl, staring at it with complete absorption. When he finally struck a match and drew the flame into the pipe, he glanced at me. A silvery cloud of smoke curled about his head and he squinted through it. "Someone doesn't want you at Harrowgate."

"But why?!"

"I'm not sure, but my guess is that you're in the way somehow. You're keeping someone from something—"

"I don't understand—"

"Neither do I but I think the danger is there nevertheless."

I stared at him. "Who are you?" Why would a stranger take such an interest in my affairs?

He sighed and puffed at the pipe. "I met your brother in South Africa."

"You know Charles—?!" Why had he made such a secret of it?! "Where is he? Why hasn't he written—"

Scofield smiled and held up a hand. "I don't know. I came here looking for him."

I chewed at my lip. "I see."

"Maybe I'd better start from the beginning."

I nodded. "That would be best."

"Charles and I met in Cape Town last year. There'd been a bit of a scrape in a local pub and a couple of fellows were roughing him up rather badly. Another chap and myself pitched in to even up the odds." He smiled briefly. "We came out of it all right but the other two didn't fare as well, I'm afraid. One died from a crack on the skull he seemed to have gotten after he left the pub. Reggie and I vouched for your brother, so there was no question of it being his doing. The police suspected the chap's own buddy, but nothing was ever proved. Charles and Reggie and I became friends. Charles was in the Army, of course, but we saw him often. He seemed to have a lot of free time, the fighting's all but done there, of course."

He puffed at the pipe. "Charles was due for a leave and Reggie was headed home about the same time. Your brother invited both of us to come to Harrowgate to visit. I must say he described the place accurately, said it was a bit run down but that he was going to set things to right as soon as he got back."

"And my grandfather—?"

"Charles claimed he'd discovered something that was going to get him welcomed with open arms and that Harrowgate would become the place it had once been."

"I don't understand—"

"I don't know any more than that. Charles had a secret, and he was as excited as a child with a toy. I had the feeling it had something to do with the fight in the pub that night we'd met, but your brother wouldn't elaborate. He had a month's leave and he planned to set things in motion—that was the way he described it. Then when he finished his tour of duty, he said he'd come back to Harrowgate and spend the rest of his life as the Lord of the Manor."

It sounded so unlike Charles, I found it difficult to believe. Charles had always been so practical, so stable. . . .

"But Charles never reported back after his leave," he said.

"What?!"

Paul Scofield shook his head and puffed silver smoke. "There was no official inquiry, what with his having only a month or two left to serve, but unless he turns himself in there may be a bit of trouble."

"He wouldn't do such a thing! There must be some mistake." Charles had left for South Africa, leaving Juliette behind at Harrowgate to await his return.

Paul Scofield sighed. "I felt the same way, and when I returned to England I began looking for him. I made discreet inquiries here and was told that he had returned to his regiment—which I knew he hadn't. So I concentrated my efforts in London. My first step was to look up Reggie and see if the two had made contact."

"And had they?"

"Reggie seemed to have vanished also. At least from London. I tracked him here."

"To Harrowgate?"

"Yes. He'd told several friends he wouldn't be coming back." His eyes hooded. "He was right about that. . . ."

"What do you mean?" I had a feeling of dread I could not explain.

"His family sent an investigator to look for him. The man reported that Reggie had stayed in the village a few nights when he arrived, asking questions and roaming about. Then he disappeared, left his baggage at the inn, but never returned for it."

I waited, unable to speak. The dread swelling inside me.

"A few weeks later, Reggie's body was found in the woods. There was no identification on him and no one came forward to claim the body . . . so he was buried and the matter closed."

I shuddered.

Paul took a deep breath. "After he'd identified the body, Ellis Simpson stayed on to try to learn what Reggie had been after."

Simpson! That was the name of the dead man who'd been discovered in the Harrowgate woods only two days ago! "Simpson was an investigator?"

I must have looked stricken, for Paul Scofield leaned forward quickly and said, "You know . . . ?"

I nodded. "The constable informed us. But

why—?" What was the dreadful secret of Harrowgate that had already claimed so many lives?!

"That's what I'm trying to find out, but so far I haven't had much luck." He stared at me, fussing with his pipe and looking thoughtful. "I hoped to spare you the ordeal of stumbling over Simpson's body . . ."

"It was you—that day in the woods—"

"Yes. I had no idea who was on the path, so I stayed out of sight. When I saw you, I wanted to make sure you didn't come across the body—and also that you were in no danger from whoever had killed Simpson."

"And when I fainted . . . ?"

"I carried you to safety, then got back to the village to report what I'd found. I was pretty sure you wouldn't venture into the woods again soon, and I didn't want to go up to the house, at least not then." He set aside his pipe. "What were you doing in the woods?"

"I went to see Annie to get a tonic for Juliette."

He nodded. "What do you know of Jonathon Newgate?"

I was surprised. "Nothing at all. I'd never laid eyes on him before that day, nor have I since. He seems to be taking good care of old Annie, and he *is* her relative . . ."

He rubbed his fist against the side of his chin. "There's talk in the village that he expected the old woman to inherit a sizable fortune from your grandfather's estate. It's possible he showed up to claim a share of it."

I recalled Jonathon speaking of my grandfather's will and the way Annie had been cut from it. But a sizable fortune? Surely Grandfather Franklin never intended more than to care for the old woman's needs—and she had been deprived of even that. But I also remembered my uneasy feeling that Jonathon Newgate had been watching me, been hostile . . .

"What about the others?" Paul asked. "Lionel Mundy and Wiley Temple?"

I blinked. "Surely you're not suggesting that either of them had anything to do with this—these—deaths?" It was too horrible to consider. "They were accidents—"

"The police aren't too sure. There were definite signs of a struggle in both instances, marks on the bodies that were inflicted before death. The police suspect foul play. Whatever it was Reggie was looking for probably cost him his life. And if Simpson got into it, it accounts for his death too."

"But what could it be? Charles wasn't here, what was Reggie after?"

"That seems to be a mystery. Neither Reggie nor I knew Charles very well. We saw him from time to time and always had a bit of fun when we did, but Reggie was often gone for long periods of time, and I had my work. There was something—" He hesitated, glancing toward the bright meadow beyond the window and sipping his tea. When he looked back to me, he said, "Reggie mentioned something about recognizing the man with whom your brother had the fight in the pub the night we met him. That seemed to surprise Charles and he didn't want to talk about it. I had the feeling that the chap was someone from the past that Charles was very surprised to run into."

"But Charles never said what the fight was about?"

He shook his head. "Claimed it was a case of mistaken identity—the man had thought he was someone else. If Reggie discovered anything on his own, he didn't tell me about it."

It was all so confusing, I could make no sense of it whatever. I finished my tea and set the cup on the small wood table that had been polished to a shine. "Thank you for everything, Mr. Scofield. I appreciate your kindness more than I can tell. I wish there were some way I could shed light on the mystery that seems to surround the death of your friend, but I am at a complete loss. If only Charles would come back I'm sure he could clear up everything quickly."

Paul Scofield's eyes clouded and his brow furrowed. "Do you know any reason why your brother would not have reported back to his regiment as he planned?"

I shook my head, feeling a cold dread inside me again. "None. He told Juliette he was sailing in a day or two and would be home to stay in only a couple of months' time. Surely if he had other plans, he would not have left her here alone—"

His frown became a scowl, and I recognized something akin to fear in his eyes.

"You don't think something has happened to him—?!" My hands trembled and I clutched them tightly in my lap. The thought had not entered my mind before. I had easily explained away Juliette's fears, confident that Charles was merely delayed . . . unavoidably. Now. . . .

He shook his head quickly. "Of course not."

But there was no conviction in his voice, and I had the sudden, horrible fear that Charles was dead.

Chapter Twelve

Paul Scofield rose from his chair and came to put a comforting hand on my shoulder. "I didn't mean to worry you. Put it from your mind now. I'll keep looking around, and I promise you'll be the first to hear if I discover anything." He smiled and it lit his handsome face. "Unless, of course, I can convince you to pack your things and leave Harrowgate."

"I can't—"

"London would be safer until we discover what's behind this."

I shook my head. "Juliette is in no condition to travel, and I will not leave her."

He looked thoughtful but did not try to persuade me. "Then you must promise not to be off roaming by yourself. Stay out of the woods and be careful until this mystery is cleared up."

I found myself nodding, chilled by the thought that unknown danger lurked about me and I was unable to determine its source. If only Charles—I caught myself abruptly. I would not think of Charles now, I could not. If anything had happened to him—

"I'll bring the trap around," he said cheerfully. "It will only take a moment."

He went out and I saw his figure pass the window as he went around the house to the small barn I'd noticed from the top of the hill. By the time he brought the horse and cart, I was waiting at the front door, anxious to be on my way—to get back to Juliette and more familiar surroundings.

We were silent during the ride, which took nearly half an hour around by the road. He pulled the cart up in front of the portico and I scrambled out before he could help me down. My conversation with him had left me strangely unnerved, unsure of anything, of whom I could trust and whom I should fear. I thanked him and went inside quickly.

Emma Mundy was in the foyer, aimlessly arranging the tray and lamp on the marble table. I knew she had been watching through the tall mullioned windows that flanked the main door, but she stared without comment as I closed the door and cut off the view of Paul Scofield leading the mare toward the stable. I hurried upstairs, still feeling her eyes on my back, and retreated to my room.

I changed from the dusty riding dress and washed up at the basin of tepid water on the commode. I brushed my hair vigorously, freeing it of bits of grass and twigs that had lodged there in my precipitous fall. Paul had dismissed the shot that caused the horse to bolt almost too easily with the idea of a poacher. It was possible of course, but I had the feeling he did not believe it any more than I. The shot had been deliberate—I was sure of it. Had it been meant for me? Or to frighten the mare as Paul said? Both ideas were terrifying, since it meant someone deliberately wanted to injure me—or worse, kill me. I'd had two accidents and either might have been fatal!

But who had known I would be on the trail? I had talked only with Mrs. Dobbs before leaving for the Rutherford cottage. Had someone overheard—or questioned the cook later? Had I been followed?

I dressed in a sprigged muslin and tied my hair back with a green ribbon, glancing in the mirror then patting my pale cheeks to bring color back to them. I walked to the window and stared at the east wing, thinking about the mysterious tapping that had drawn me there last night. Was someone hiding in the unused portion of the house—a stranger who might wish me harm? Was someone looking for something? What?

I considered the story Paul Scofield had told me of Charles' encounters in South Africa and the excitement with which he returned to Harrowgate. Was there a connection? Reggie had followed Charles' path—and died—as had the investigator who followed him. Surely there had to be a connection. And whatever it was, Charles' secret lay at the root of it.

I went along the hall to Juliette's room only to find her napping, so I closed the door silently. I couldn't help noting that she looked much better. The terrible pallor was gone and her face had lost the pinched, tired look it had when I first came. Annie's tonic, and perhaps my presence, were speeding her recovery.

With a glance at the stairwell, I walked toward the far end of the hall and the door to the east wing. It was closed, locked, with the key hanging in its accustomed place. Who had locked it after my flight last night? I unlocked it and slipped the key into the pocket of my dress, shutting the door softly behind me. In daylight, the deserted wing did not hold the terrors and shadows it had before. I had to learn the secret of the room.

Dusty patterns of sunlight filtered through the long windows along the hall, clearly showing the double path of my footprints in the dust—and no others. The east wing smelled musty and slightly mildewed, and grotesque patterns on the ceilings and walls showed where moisture had seeped in over the years. If Charles planned to restore Harrowgate, perhaps he would reopen the wing, or tear it down. It was foolish to let it decay like this.

I found the lamp I had left near the bedroom door, and the charred match with which I'd tried to relight it. The floor was scuffed and the dust so much disturbed that it was impossible to tell if footsteps other than my own had marked it. Tracks of small rodents crisscrossed in every direction, making me shudder again.

I opened the door to the bedroom—sure that I had not stopped to close it in my hasty flight last night. The room was not empty of furniture as I had supposed. A high postered bed stood at one wall, the canopy tattered and hanging in wisps of rotted lace, the spread grey with dust and age. A highboy dresser had been pulled out from the wall, the drawers yanked open, yawning emptily. Irregular swatches of wallpaper had been ripped from the walls, exposing the bare wood beneath. In several places holes had been gouged in the wood, boards ripped from the studs!

I moved about, glancing at the fantastic damage that had been done, unable to comprehend why anyone would vandalize property in such a way. Dust covers, pulled from furniture, were pushed in an untidy heap in a corner. A small chair was overturned, its cloth bottom slashed and the stuffing removed.

The only explanation was that someone was searching for something—something small enough to be hidden in an inconspicuous place. The nightly tappings, the lights, were the stealthy search—for what?

I returned to the hall, opening doors of other rooms and finding the same destruction everywhere. The entire upper floor of the east wing had been ransacked—apparently in vain since the midnight searcher had still been at his task last night.

I was angry enough to forget my fears. Why had the Mundys not heard any of the noise and investigated? How long had the mysterious searching been going on—and why?

I stood at the top of the curving stairway leading to the lower floor. Was it my imagination or were the steps remarkably free of dust? Had they been used regularly? I took a deep breath and started down, my hand on the rail to steady myself since my knees felt suddenly weak. I knew I was being foolish wandering about alone but I had to know if the lower rooms of the east wing had also been searched.

The lower hall had once been magnificent. Even now, the sunlight caught the prisms of the huge dusty chandelier that hung in the foyer and sent rainbows of light dancing about the walls. I concentrated, trying to recall the layout of the rooms. It had been a long time since Charles and I had ventured here, and my memories were dim. The ballroom opened off to the right, I was sure, and I saw the ornate carved doors, closed now, with their brass dragon-shaped handles dull and unpolished. My movement through the hall caused the teardrop crystals of the chandelier to sway slightly, and they tinkled one against the other. I felt drawn toward the ballroom, crossing the hall and putting my hand to the curved twin handles. They moved readily under my touch and the heavy doors swung open. The current of air made the prisms chime again . . . almost like the sound of distant instruments. I stood transfixed, mesmerized by the magic of the room and the distinct impression of music. A faraway stringed quartet . . . a haunting waltz . . .

Suddenly, I was no longer in a dusty, forgotten room. I could hear the music clearly now and shadowy figures moved about the room in time to it. A ball was in progress. . . .

A smiling girl in a blue gown danced by in the arms of a soldier in tight white breeches, a red coat with green facings and brass buttons. He had eyes for no one but her as they glided past, twirling and laughing as the girl held one side of her skirt with a free hand, exposing dainty blue slippers that matched the gown. Other couples moved past as the music swelled above the sound of merriment. Then I saw Elizabeth Ashcroft and the young man I'd seen with her in the bedroom, her bridegroom. Harland was gazing at Elizabeth with such adoration that I felt their love and happiness radiate around me. Elizabeth was wearing the cream-coloured dress of the portrait, the green ribbons trailing and fluttering at her bosom and waist. The low neckline showed her bare shoulders, her skin only a shade paler than the colour of the gown. About her throat she wore a dazzling pendant, the diamond winking and gleaming in the light. The matching ring glittered on her finger.

The music stopped and the sound of voices and laughter seemed to fade with it. Once more I found myself watching only the young lovers. They came toward me and instinctively I stepped aside to let them pass. The figures were so real that I almost reached out to touch what must be human flesh, yet there was no sound of their steps on the parquet floor or on the marble as they crossed the foyer and climbed the stairs, hand in hand. Elizabeth glanced over her shoulder, toward the ballroom, and smiled conspiratorially. They were stealing away from the party—wanting to be alone.

Still in a dream-like daze, I followed them, drawn by impulses I could not explain nor understand. It was as though I were a witness to the scene for a purpose—seeing a performance that was for my benefit alone.

At the head of the stairs, they turned toward the bedroom where I'd encountered the mysterious apparition last night. They glided through the door as though it stood open, and I found my hand trembling as I turned the knob and stood in the doorway, watching and waiting, ready to flee if I were to become witness to a romantic interlude. The heavy feeling of unseen danger still filled me, and I could not force myself to turn away.

The young couple stopped abruptly, staring at a third figure who stood near the highboy. It was the man who had threatened Harland in the ghostly scene I'd witnessed last night in the hall. The furniture in the room was still in disarray but the couple seemed not to notice and moved about as though the room were as they always knew it. The girl looked annoyed to find the man there and somewhat surprised. Her bridegroom looked angry. He crossed to the other with quick strides, his mouth working as he vented his anger with words I could not hear. Elizabeth looked stricken, her eyes flitting from her husband to the other man. He was obviously not a stranger to her, and I had the feeling that in other circumstances she might be pleased to see him—but not now—not when she had stolen a few moments from the ball to be with her love.

The two men were arguing again, their faces and gestures angry. In the ghostly pallor of the sunlight filtering through the dusty windows, I could see the other man more clearly now. He was someone I'd never seen before, yet I had the uncanny feeling that I should know him—that he resembled someone I had seen or known recently.

Elizabeth Ashcroft ran to her husband and pulled at his arm, beseeching him with silent words. He looked both ashamed and frightened as he met her glance and spoke softly to her. The other man laughed and said something that made Elizabeth turn and strike out at him. The soundless slap of her hand against his face was so vicious it made me recoil, but the man only laughed and pointed to the jewels at her throat and hand.

For a moment the tableau was frozen in

that instant of horror. Then without another word, Elizabeth reached up and unclasped the pendant, pulled the ring from her finger. She flung both at the man's outstretched hand then turned and fled past me along the hall to a back stairway and vanished in the dusty gloom beyond the windows. The bridegroom grabbed for the other man, scuffling and trying to recover his wife's jewels, but the other shoved him aside, knocking him to the floor. Before Harland could gain his feet, the man had run from the room and vanished down the stairs where the girl had gone. The dazed bridegroom struggled to his feet and staggered after them.

The hall was silent and empty, and I was staring at shadows and distorted rays of afternoon sunlight, shortening now as the day faded.

Chapter Thirteen

I don't know how long I stood in the dim hall, surrounded by a feeling of dread that had pervaded the scene I'd witnessed. What I had seen was a reenactment of part of the story Becky had told me—the quarrel between the young couple, the missing jewels . . . But who was the other man, the one who had demanded and taken the necklace and ring? There had been no mention of him in Becky's tale, or any other that I had ever heard.

The missing jewels had caused two deaths—perhaps more. Elizabeth had fled the house and been lost in the marsh; her father, blaming Harland, had killed the young man in a fit of rage, and the legend of the curse of Harrowgate was born.

And none of it was true—at least none of the facts that placed the blame on young Harland Beaumont. Someone else had taken the jewels—someone else had escaped the house and made off with them.

I felt a chill suddenly, as though a draft swept me. I shivered and hurried my footsteps along the hall toward the main wing. I could not shake the feeling that the missing jewels were somehow connected with the strange occurrences that were taking place at Harrowgate now. Did someone believe they were here? Was that the reason for the search, the ransacking of the upper rooms and the prowling and tapping I'd seen and heard? More important, had Grandfather Franklin been aware of it? Was that why he prowled about and refused to tell anyone what he was looking for?

But surely the jewels could not have been here all the years since Elizabeth Ashcroft thrust them at the man who had made off with them. Why would Grandfather Franklin believe they had?

Charles!

Charles had told Paul Scofield he was going to restore Harrowgate to its former grandeur, that he'd discovered something that was going to insure his welcome here.

The missing jewels? But how? I wasn't even sure Charles knew the legend of the gems. If we'd heard it as children I'd forgotten it until Becky retold it. Even if Charles *did* know the story, what possible clue might he have uncovered to the whereabouts of the jewels? He'd spent the last three years in the Army, moving from place to place, seemingly caring little for the past he'd left behind.

I shook my head impatiently, not able to figure out the meanings of these strange happenings or how they affected my life. I had no doubt that they did—everything that had happened at Harrowgate since my arrival pointed to the fact that all was not as it seemed. But Charles had no connections with diamonds— not unless he had come across the missing jewels in South Africa. After all these years, that seemed unlikely.

In my own room, I stood gazing out the window, letting my thoughts wander, trying to form sensible patterns. Paul said Reggie recognized the man with whom Charles had fought that night in the tavern. It was possible that he might know people in the area connected with diamonds—even stolen diamonds such as Elizabeth Ashcroft's!

Had Charles recognized the missing gems, somehow found a way to get them and bring them back to Harrowgate where they rightfully belonged? It seemed far fetched, but it could be an explanation.

That would mean that the diamonds were here now. Charles had hidden them at Harrowgate until he could return and take over the management of the estate. Had Grandfather Franklin known, or suspected? His nocturnal wanderings had been a fruitless search for something, so, perhaps, Charles had not told him the exact location of the jewels, only that he had recovered them.

But someone else knew too. The mysterious man who held secret conferences with Wiley Temple, and who ransacked the east wing in his own search. If both grandfather and the trespasser concentrated their search in the east wing, it seemed likely they had some evidence that Charles had hidden the jewels there.

But where?

I sighed. I seemed to go round and round in circles without ever finding a solution, only more questions. If I could identify the man I'd seen scuffling with Harland Beaumont and making off with Elizabeth's necklace and ring, I might have something to go on. I had not been able to shake the feeling that he was somehow familiar . . . Was the dark young man a member of the family?

I could not rest until I found out. I left my room and headed downstairs for the library. The house was quiet, with no one about in the halls. The sky beyond the windows was graying as the sun dipped behind the hill and cast long shadows along the eastern exposure of Harrowgate. I had not seen Mrs. Mundy since my encounter with her in the hall when Paul brought me home in the trap; and I had not seen Lionel at all. What did the two do to occupy their time in the big house? How little I knew about them, and how willing I had been to accept their presence without question.

I wished Wiley were here. There were so many questions he might answer for me—or was it that I missed him? The house was strangely empty without him, and I realized all at once how much his presence had come to mean to me. Somehow I was sure he played no part in the strange happenings at Harrowgate. Perhaps, like me, he was trying to get at the truth but did not want to accuse the Mundys unfairly. As soon as he returned, I would tell him everything I had learned and admit my suspicions. Together we might find explanations for what seemed inexplicable.

The library smelled of old leather and hidden dust. I suspected that the books had not been removed from the shelves for a thorough housecleaning since my grandfather lost the ability to oversee such tasks. How well I recalled the room and the hours I'd spent here as a child, whiling away my loneliness and losing myself in volumes that let my imagination soar to faraway places. I had buried myself in novels, in biographies of people who had conquered worlds that seemed so distant.

Charles, on the other hand, had soaked up the past and present as though his appetite could never be satisfied. He poured over books of armies and soldiers, reliving wars and history that had been the foundation of England and of Harrowgate itself. I recalled his excitement when he discovered some ancient hand-written volumes that charted the history of Harrowgate from its earliest times, and his total absorption with the faded daguerreotypes he discovered tucked between the pages of some of the later pages of the book.

It had to be here somewhere. I closed my eyes and tried to visualize the size and shape of the book, but the mental picture would not come. I had not paid enough attention for details to impress themselves on my memory.

I made a slow circle of the room, pausing to glance at titles, occasionally pulling down a volume that looked promising. It took me almost twenty minutes to find the one I wanted, and I carried it to the seat built into the huge bay window facing the drive. I sat and opened the book on my lap.

The edges of the pages were yellowed with age and brittle and broken at some of the corners. The inked words in cursive script had paled with the years but were still legible. I scanned the pages, checking dates until I came to the first set of daguerreotypes inserted between the pages. I peered at the stern face of the man pictured. An Ashcroft, without doubt. I glanced at the reverse side. *Damon Ashcroft, 1849.* Elizabeth's father. I studied the picture again and wondered where it had been taken, but the background was unidentifiable. Quickly I went through the others. Damon and a woman in white, his bride. Damon with a young child beside him. Some of the later pictures were not as indistinct, and I studied them carefully. They chronicled Elizabeth's life from childhood to a young woman. One showed Elizabeth and a young man whom I recognized immediately as Harland. I wondered if it had marked the occasion of their engagement. In the background, several people were grouped, smiling at the camera but slightly out of focus as the lens was directed at the young couple. Still, their faces could be made out. I tried to identify them. One woman wore a servant's white apron.

Holding the picture to the light, I examined it closely. It had been taken fifty years ago, yet I could not mistake Annie Newgate as a young girl. Her bony features were distinct, her shoulders slightly stooped even as I remembered them in my own childhood. And close beside her, his arm lightly at her waist, was a young man—the same one I'd already seen in the ghostly scenes with Harland and Elizabeth!

I slipped the picture into my pocket and closed the book, carrying it to the shelf and replacing it. I had found the answer I was searching for—at least in part. The man, whoever he was, was someone familiar with the house, part of the staff, probably, since he had stood in the background with the servants.

With the suddenness of a bolt of lightning, I realized why the stranger had seemed familiar! He resembled Jonathon Newgate—without the heavy mustache and a few years older, but the face was the same! If Jonathon Newgate was related to old Annie, it probably meant the young man in the picture was too.

I turned at a small sound behind me, my heart pounding with fright since I had believed myself alone. Becky was peering at me from the doorway, head tilted inquisitively.

"Would you like me to light the lamps, Miss?"

"No, I was just going upstairs . . ." I walked toward the door, glancing at the lengthening shadows beyond the windowpane and noticing that Becky had her cape about her shoulders, ready to leave for the day. I smiled and she smiled shyly in return. "Miss Juliette is looking ever so much better since you've come, Miss Margaret. It's such a pleasure to see her up and about."

"She's up now?" I asked, surprised and strangely alarmed at the thought that Juliette might undertake too much too soon.

Becky's head bobbed. "Yes, Miss. I just helped her to the chair by the window so's she c'n wave as I go down the drive."

I smiled again. "Then you'd best not keep her waiting or she'll worry what's happened to you. I'll see you tomorrow, Becky."

She glanced about the darkening library and seemed to shiver. I thought of the picture in my pocket. Perhaps Becky would be able to give me some details about old Annie—

"Becky?"

"Yes, Miss?" She turned in the doorway, the soft glow of the hall lamp behind her putting her face in shadows.

"You know Annie Newgate, don't you?"

"To be sure, Miss. Everyone in Louthwick knows old Annie."

"Does she have a family, or did she at one time?"

Becky's head moved in a solemn nod. "Annie's husband was crushed by a felled tree in the old woods. Left her with a young son to raise alone." She hesitated, but I could not read the expression on her face.

"What happened to him?"

She shook her head. "Poor Annie . . . the boy turned out lazy and worthless. Drinking and gambling . . . Several times he was caught stealing bits of silver or small valuables from the house. 'Tis said the master would have put him in gaol but for Annie. She was a good woman, and a hard worker. So Anthony was sent off to London, never to set foot in Harrowgate again."

"But he visited his mother?"

"I don't know, Miss. More'n likely, knowing how Annie doted on him, but I don't think she'd let him in the house." Becky shook her head. "She was too loyal to the master."

"Was there never any news of him? Did anyone in the village hear—"

"Not that I know of. Of course, that was a long time ago." She glanced surreptitiously toward the growing darkness beyond the windows.

"Thank you, Becky. You'd best be on your way now."

"Thank you, Miss." She bobbed and scurried toward the door, and I stood at the mullioned windows and watched her hurry down the drive. Apparently she made the trip to and from town each day on foot, but had no fear once she passed the woods of Har-rowgate.

I climbed the stairs and paused at Juliette's door, where a thin shaft of light showed under it. I knocked softly.

"Margaret! I'm so glad you came up—oh, I feel so much better. It seems absolutely sinful to loll about like this doing nothing." She was sitting at the small desk near the window, a large-globed lamp lighting the letter she'd been writing. She laid the pen aside with a smile. "To Charles . . ." Her smile faded. "Oh, how I do wish I would hear from him!"

"There now, don't start worrying again. And you mustn't overtire yourself—"

"I feel fine, really I do. It's almost as though I've come out of a fog of some kind, suddenly everything seems so much brighter and clearer since you arrived. Ever since Grandfather Franklin died, I was in a daze, almost as though I were drugged. It was so difficult to think, and I kept imagining I heard voices."

That startled me. "What kind of voices?"

She shrugged and pulled her robe about her shoulders, holding it at her throat and frown-ing. "That's just it, I don't remember. It was all so fuzzy and I got so weak."

"Well, you're better now, and you'll be stronger each day. Perhaps when you are well enough, we'll go to London, the two of us." I was thinking of Paul's warning.

Her eyes went wide. "But I promised

Charles I'd wait here."

"Surely he wouldn't object to a few days shopping?"

She laughed. "No, of course not. It *would* be fun. It's been a long time since I've been anywhere."

"It's settled then. All you must do is get well and strong."

"I shall, you'll see." She looked radiant.

"I must change for dinner. Don't tire yourself. . . ."

In my own room, I lighted the lamp, noting that the second lamp that I had left in the east wing was now back in its accustomed place on the table. The key, which I had removed from my pocket, lay beside it. A mute testimony to my own excursion to the east wing. Yet no one had mentioned it . . . Again, the veil of secrecy surrounding the old wing angered and frightened me. Whatever was happening there, the Mundys had to be party to it, I was sure.

At dinner I confronted them with the question. "Did one of you bring the lamp in my room back from the east wing?"

The couple glanced at each other and Emma looked away, letting her husband answer.

"Yes. I noticed the door was open and went to check. When I saw the lamp, I recognized it of course. What in the world were you doing in that part of the house? It's dangerous— some of those old boards are nearly rotted through. You might have had a nasty accident."

"I was disturbed during the night by hammering sounds and I went to investigate. I don't understand why neither of you has been aware of them before. Have you seen the destruction that's been done there?"

Lionel frowned, unable to deny his knowledge since he'd admitted being there.

"Vandals . . . kids from town. Damn shame. I'll speak to the constable."

"The townspeople are afraid to come anywhere near Harrowgate after dark. They say it's haunted," I challenged.

Emma chewed at her lip and toyed with food. Lionel glared at me. "If you're saying that me and Emma are somehow responsible—"

"I didn't say that, but I do think something should have been done long before the matter got to this stage. The rooms are a shambles, almost a total loss."

"Never been used for these past fifty years . . . don't see what it matters," Emma mumbled.

"But Charles has plans to restore it—" Their heads came up so suddenly I quickly realized I had admitted knowledge they were not aware I had. I cut a piece of roast and lifted my fork. "Well, we must at least take pains to see that no further damage is done. I shall call to the village and have a locksmith come out and change all the locks." I looked at Lionel. "Can you hire someone to board over the windows so they are sealed?"

He nodded, and we dropped the subject, eating our meal in silence until it was interrupted by the peal of the bell. Emma looked up, startled, as Lionel pushed back his chair and left the dining room. He returned a few moments later with a letter which he handed to me.

"The Riker lad from the village brought it for you, said it was important." He was staring at me curiously.

I held the envelope, staring at the unfamiliar childish scrawl, until Lionel had resumed his seat. I tore the envelope and drew out the single sheet.

"Miss Margaret—Old Annie says she *must* see you—it's very important. Mum thinks she may be dyin.'" It was signed "Becky."

I recalled now her name was Riker—and somehow she had managed to convince her brother to deliver the message. She would not do it unless it were imperative.

"What is it? Has something happened?"

I looked up at the watchful faces. "I must go to Annie Newgate's cottage," I said.

"Now?" Emma looked shocked, glancing toward the window over which the curtains had been drawn for the night.

Remembering the terrifying woods and the equally terrifying accident with the carriage, I was not anxious to try either again, but Becky's message was so urgent—and she had somehow overcome her own terror and that of her brother in order to deliver it. I had to go—now.

"Can you take me around by carriage?" I asked Lionel.

"It's not fixed yet. I haven't been able to get the part I need—"

"But you took Wiley to the station—" I insisted.

He glanced sidelong at his wife. "I hired a carriage from the village. If you like, I can ride in and—"

"No, there isn't time," I insisted. Remembering my recent promise to Paul Scofield and my earlier one to Wiley, I took a deep breath. "Will you lead me through the woods?" The very thought terrified me, but at least I would not be alone.

Lionel was silent a moment, then nodded reluctantly. "I'll fetch a lantern."

I dashed upstairs and quickly changed the soft slippers I was wearing for sturdy shoes. I wrapped my heavy cloak around my shoulders. Descending, I wished fervently that there were some way I might communicate with Paul Scofield so he could accompany me on this mission. But Becky's note had sounded so urgent, there was no time to lose.

Lionel was waiting in the hall. Moments later, Emma pulled open the heavy front doors and I stepped out into the damp, dark night.

Chapter Fourteen

The lantern cast a pale yellow frame of light about us as Lionel led the way down the drive and around the base of the hill. The gentle slope of the meadow seemed steeper now, and the grass was slippery with dew. As we went lower into the valley, the mist swirled and eddied around our feet, thickening and rising as we reached the plateau of the woods. The sky was dark despite the cloudless day, and the damp air portended more rain. I hugged my cloak close and hurried to keep up with Lionel.

He'd said nothing since we left the house. Now he turned, lifting the lantern as though to inspect my face and see if I was determined to go on. I nodded impatiently, forcing myself not to shudder at the thought of the black woods. Lionel's face seemed strangely cold in the pale yellow blur of the lantern; he turned away and started out again, more slowly now as he picked his way carefully along the winding path.

The woods by daylight had been dismal and scarey, but in the darkness of night they were terrifying. I tried to keep my gaze off the grotesquely shaped trees that seemed to reach boney fingers toward me. The light glittered from time to time on the dark pools of slimy water, and bits of leaves and branches crunched under Lionel's heavy steps, sounding like shots cracking in the silence. I kept my eyes on his heels and the dancing circle of light, trying to step where he stepped. I was breathless and found it hard to keep up.

"Don't go so fast—" I called to him. He seemed not to hear as he crashed ahead, the light growing smaller as the darkness closed between us.

"Wait!" My demand was a breathless whisper, and the light became a winking pinpoint which vanished among the trees ahead of me.

I tried to run after him, but I stumbled and fell to my knees. For a moment, panic filled me so completely that I felt soundless screams rising in my throat. I scrambled to my feet and stood where I was, trying to orient myself. The swampy ground was a menace on every side; if I stepped off the path, I might sink into one of the dark pools. It was impossible to see, the darkness was so complete now.

I reached out, searching with my hands for a solid tree on which to lean, finding only thorny brambles that cut my flesh. I forced myself to breathe deeply, counting silently and slowly until I knew my voice would come back. Then, with another breath, I cupped my hands to my mouth and called.

"Lionel!"

The sound echoed around me, seeming hollow in the vast woods. I held my breath, listening and waiting for an answer. When none came, I called again.

"Lionel!"

The sound died and the silence closed around me once more. He was too far ahead to hear. The thick growth of trees and shrubs blanketed my voice, limiting it to only a close range. But surely Lionel would turn around and see that I was no longer behind him. He would come back in search of me. . . .

My heart pounded against my ribs. Suppose he didn't! I had done what Paul had warned me about—I had let myself be drawn into the perilous woods again. I could not blunder about the marsh without a light to guide me, but neither could I stay here and wait for whatever might come.

Panic seized me, and I wanted to run. With greatest effort I forced myself to move forward slowly and cautiously, testing the earth before each step. The path was firm, but the marsh around it was spongy, then soggy as it rimmed the murky pools. Each time my shoe encountered a soft spot, I drew back, my heart hammering beneath my ribs. Several times, sharp branches of trees slashed at my face and clothes. Vines tried to entwine me; once I bumped into a gnarled tree that seemed for a moment like someone grabbing me.

I stifled a scream. Tears were running down my cheeks now, and I could taste the salty blood where I had bitten my lip in confusion and terror. Why had Lionel been so thought-less, running ahead and leaving me to flounder in the darkness? He should have known how easily I might get lost.

I stopped. abruptly, my knees weak and pulse racing. Had he wanted me to be lost in the deadly swamp? Was Lionel the one I had to fear? Had I let him lead me into a trap?

I heard a crash in the brush somewhere close by. Wildly, I searched for the telltale light of the lantern, but there was nothing but blackness, intense and cloying. I heard the sound again, sure now that it was a heavy footfall. I plunged ahead, almost running, bouncing off brush and trees and sobbing be-tween gasps of breath. I had lost direction completely, and suddenly the ground beneath my feet was no longer solid. Panting, I tried to find the path again but splashed through shallow pools of water, slipping and sliding on the mucky bottom. The water became deeper, dragging at my cloak and soaking through my shoes, chilling my feet. I floundered onto a hummock and clambered onto it and sat pant-ing. Fear prickled at my hair roots and I shivered with a new chill.

I saw the glimmer of light then and cried out with relief. Lionel had returned! The lantern winked in and out of trees less than a hundred yards from me.

"Lionel! I'm here—"

There was no answer, but my relief at seeing the light was so enormous that I didn't care.

"Over here. Thank heaven you've come . . ." I was sobbing, struggling to my feet, trying to stay on the swaying hummock of dry ground. The light moved to the right, then up. It swayed slightly then came to rest, a beacon showing me the way to safety. I lifted my soggy cloak and walked slowly toward it.

The ground was soft again almost immediately. But with the light so close, it had to be the shortest and safest direction to the path. The mist that had been invisible in the darkness was now a gray shroud rising from the marsh. At times it obscured the lantern glow momentarily and new panic filled me, but I plunged ahead.

Quite suddenly, I saw a figure—not Lionel but the white apparition that had twice before warned me of danger. It was clearer this time, closer, so that I could see the old man's features under the mass of white hair and beard. His eyes seemed to bore through me, stern but without anger. A thin wavering hand raised and pointed to my left. Grandfather Franklin was warning me back, insisting that I go in the opposite direction—even though the lantern was ahead of me.

I took a tentative step toward him and the

misty figure surged toward me, the stern face scowling. I realized at once that my foot had slipped into deeper water—that I was on the brink of a deep pool! I stumbled backwards, pulling my foot and shoe from the slime and groping for the hummock I had used as a resting place. When I found it, I moved past it, following the command of the silent ghostly figure who pointed the way.

Within minutes, the ground under my feet became firmer. Then I was on the path! I sprawled flat, weeping and laughing at the same time, gasping for breath. When I finally pulled myself up and looked about, the apparition had vanished.

Once more Grandfather Franklin had saved me! I sobbed with relief and inspected my surroundings. I could still see the dim glow of the lantern across the marsh. Obviously it had been hung on a low branch to lure me toward it—directly into the dangerous pool that might well have claimed my life. By its feeble glow, I could see that the path made a loop, skirting the pool and its danger.

Almost crawling on hands and knees, I made my way to the lantern and lifted it from the stub of a branch. Holding it ahead of me, I followed the path easily, noting a few familiar landmarks that told me I was almost at the clearing where Annie's house was. I ran the last yards, anxious to be out of the woods at last and vowing never to set foot in them again!

A light burned in the cottage but no one answered my knock; I turned the knob and let myself in. I left the lantern on the table by the door, brushing my dress and cloak as best I could; they were soaked to the waist, and I could do little more than smooth them flat.

My shoes squished wetly as I crossed the tiny parlour and pulled aside the curtain of the bedroom. The old woman lay, eyes closed, thin hands atop the coverlet, fingers entwined in the cloth.

"Annie?" I whispered her name.

Her eyes opened instantly and she peered toward me. I moved closer that she might recognize me. Her lips moved soundlessly, but I saw instantly that the vacant look had vanished from her watery gray eyes. She was lucid, and she recognized me.

I smiled. "It's Margaret. I got your message . . ."

The thin head moved slightly and she moistened her dry lips with a pale tongue. "Franklin is gone . . ." she said. The words were barely a breath from her mouth.

I nodded, not sure why she had summoned me here to tell me something I already knew. Her gray eyes found mine and held my gaze. "Harrowgate is yours . . . he wanted it that way . . ." She sighed, as though the effort of talking was almost too much for her.

"But Charles—" The words escaped my lips before I could stop them.

Her old eyes filled with terror. "Dead . . .

gone . . . Harrowgate is yours."

I gasped. "Charles . . . dead?" My worst fears were confirmed by the old woman's vision.

"You must be careful," Annie whispered. "Death still walks the grounds of Harrowgate. Do not be deceived by those who would be your friends." She glanced around the tiny room as though fearful of being overheard. "You must go before it is too late. He will know!"

"Who—who?" Her fear was so real I felt it myself and found myself glancing over my shoulder. She was terrified, yet she had brought me here to warn me.

"The letter—I put it in the tiger's den—"

A sudden sound came from the parlour as the door opened. Annie's fingers clutched mine for an instant, pressing as hard as her feeble strength allowed. "He left them there for you," she whispered. Had I not been bending over her I would have not heard the words at all, so faint were they. Her grip on my hand relaxed and her eyes closed. I straightened as Jonathon Newgate appeared in the doorway. He looked at the old woman, then scowled at me.

"What are you doing here?"

I was taken aback by his surly manner, but I managed a small smile. "I heard Annie was feeling worse and stopped by to see if there was anything I could do."

He stepped back into the parlour, reeling

slightly, and I realized he'd been drinking. I hurried from the bedroom, anxious now to get away from him, but he blocked my passage. He gripped my shoulder painfully with a huge hand and surveyed my damp and dirty outfit.

"You came through the woods in the dark—all alone?" He sneered.

"No," I said, pulling free. "Lionel brought me. I had the misfortune to slip into a small pool—"

He laughed rudely. "And where is Lionel now?" I could smell the sour odor of whiskey on his breath as he came close again.

I stood my ground, trying to bluff until I could get past him and reach the door. "Outside—he said he'd wait outside—"

Jonathon laughed again, staggering back slightly off balance. I seized the opportunity to rush for the door, snatching up the lantern from the table and dashing from the cottage.

No matter what, I could not go back into the woods! I turned toward the road and rushed into the darkness, the lantern swinging against my wet cloak so that the cloth sizzled on the hot glass. I held it aloft, turning once to look back over my shoulder and see Jonathon stagger from the doorway and come after me. In spite of his drunkenness, he moved swiftly and was already closing the distance between us. I might have a chance if I blew out the lantern, but then my progress would be impeded by the darkness. The mist had turned to a fine rain now and I felt it on my hair and face.

I was unfamiliar with the road, and several times I veered off into the grass, stumbling and dragging myself to my feet as quickly as I could.

Behind me, Jonathon roared drunkenly. "You won't get away with them, I won't let you—Jus' like that high and mighty brother of yours—"

Charles! I almost stopped in my tracks with surprise. The meaning of Annie's words dawned on me suddenly. She had been warning me against Jonathon! Her own nephew—and she had been afraid that he would return and overhear. She was afraid of *him!* Because she knew he had killed Charles!

Jonathon was dangerously close now. I was exhausted, heaving for breath, each one a painful scar in my lungs and throat. I could not outrun him—so I turned to face him. I stopped so abruptly he slowed warily, eying me, then advanced, arms out like a huge bear.

"Now you're bein' smart. No sense trying to run from me no more. We'll go together—and you'll show me where your fool of a brother hid those diamonds—"

I flung the lantern with all my might, swinging it in a wide arc then letting go so it hit him hard in the chest. The force was little more than surprise, but the glass of the lantern shattered against the metal buttons of his coat and oil spattered his clothing, quickly igniting. In seconds he was engulfed in the flames, beating at them with both hands, falling to the ground and rolling in the mud, swearing loudly.

I ran pell-mell, as fast as my legs would carry me, lifting my wet cloak and skirt to my knees so that they would not slow me. I dared not pause to look back. I had done him no permanent damage, I was sure, and it was only a matter of time until he would be after me again. And when he caught me, there would be no escape this time.

Chapter Fifteen

The road had become muddy from the rain that was falling steadily now. When I first glimpsed the speck of light, I thought my mind was playing tricks on me—then I remembered the fork in the road where the Rutherford cottage stood. Paul!

I cried his name aloud into the night and raced for the light. I stumbled and fell, dragged myself to my feet again. I was unable to tell if Jonathon was in pursuit—the pounding of my pulse was too loud in my own ears. I was on the cottage path then, beating at the door, weeping hysterically.

The door opened and I stumbled into Paul's arms.

"What in God's name—?!" He pulled me inside and shut the door, half carrying me toward the fireplace where a cheery fire glowed with warmth.

"What happened? Where in the world have you been?" He pulled the armchair close to the fire and sat me in it, unmindful of my soaked clothing.

"Jonathon—he's after me—he killed Charles—"

Paul stared at me with a puzzled frown, then whirled as the front door slammed open and Jonathon filled the doorway. His wet hair was plastered to his head, slashing across his forehead like twin devil horns. The front of his coat was singed and torn. His face was black with rage and soot, his hands covered with mud. He snarled and lurched toward me.

I screamed, but Paul was between us, hitting Jonathon a blow that reeled him back against the door. The rage and the rain had sobered Jonathon some, and he came back fighting like an animal. They crashed against a table, sending several books and a small easel crashing to the floor. Jonathon crouched and came in for a new attack. He was strong and quick, but Paul's mind was clearer. Paul sidestepped quickly, and by the time Jonathon had turned and found his range again, Paul slammed another heavy blow at the other's temple. Jonathon fell to his knees, tried to get up, only to meet Paul's fist again. Jonathon seemed to hang in mid-air for a moment, then thudded to the floor in a heap.

Paul stepped over him and closed the door, then came back to me. "Now, tell me what this is all about."

Half crying, I managed to relate the story of the message from Becky and my journey through the woods to see Annie. When I told how Jonathon had tried to grab me, Paul's face darkened and he glanced at the unconscious man on the floor. When I had finished, Paul was silent for a long time.

"Everyone was so willing to accept him as genuine when he came to take care of Annie . . ." Paul said thoughtfully.

I remembered the picture in the album and quickly told Paul about it. He nodded. "Anthony might be his grandfather. I always had the feeling Jonathon was not the farm boy he pretends." He got up and crossed the room to rummage in a box and bring out a length of heavy cord. Then he bent over Jonathon to tie his hands securely behind his back and knot the other end of the rope about his ankles.

"That should hold him until the constable gets here. I'll have to ride to the village."

Panic assailed me at the thought of being left alone with the man who had tried to kill me, even though he was securely bound. Paul noted my shudder and crossed to take me in his arms. I shivered again, then drew away as thoughts of Wiley flooded. Flushing, I could not meet Paul's puzzled gaze. Abruptly, he turned toward the door and returned with a dark slicker from a peg. He wrapped it about my shoulders and drew the hood of my cape up over my wet hair. Donning a heavy jacket and cap, he lighted a lantern then led me out to a small barn where he quickly hitched the horse to the trap and helped me in.

In the dim light of the lantern, his gaze was unreadable. "It will be a wet ride, I'm afraid, but you can change into dry things as soon as you're home."

Home . . . Harrowgate was mine, Annie said. Charles was dead. . . . I felt my tears mingle with the rain as Paul drove the cart along the road toward Harrowgate.

We drew up in front of the house some minutes later, and I was surprised to find the lower floor of the house ablaze with lights. Had something happened? Juliette!

I leaped from the cart as soon as Paul had brought it to a halt and raced for the door. It opened before I could reach it, and Emma Mundy peered out. Paul came up behind me and ushered me in.

"Oh—it's you—I thought—" The woman's face was pale and worried. Her eyes were huge and filled with fear.

"Where is Lionel?" Paul demanded.

Emma's mouth fell open and she looked from one to the other of us. She was shaking and looked ready to faint. "He was with you . . ." The words held the full tone of the woman's terror.

"No, Emma, he abandoned me in the swamp to perish!" I was angry, yet I felt sorry for the pitiful woman before me. Her expression indicated that I was right—and that she had known of the plan all along. Lionel Mundy had deliberately taken me through the swamp and tried to kill me.

Emma Mundy seemed to crumple all at once, her face sagging, her eyes overflowing with tears. "He's dead—Oh Lord, he's dead!!" She began to weep hysterically. Paul moved to her and gripped her shoulders, shaking her until she stopped crying and would listen to him.

"Why were you trying to kill Margaret?"

When she didn't answer immediately, he shook her again.

She sobbed. "He said Harrowgate would come to us."

"Who said that?" Paul demanded in a low whisper.

She sniffled pitifully. "Wiley Temple."

My heart wrenched with pain. I shook my head. "Wiley—?"

"It was his idea—all of it. With you out of the way, he had a will to show we would inherit the house."

I stared at her, heartsick that I had let myself be so duped. I had foolishly believed Wiley was romantically interested in me, and I had let my heart rule my head. Weakly, I said, "You *knew* Charles was dead?"

"We had nothing to do with that, I swear! It was Jonathon and Mr. Temple. They planned the whole thing because they wanted the diamonds."

She was so frightened, I knew it was impossible for her to lie now. Paul swore softly under his breath. He came and put his arms around me. For a moment, I let myself be lost in his strength, for I had none of my own.

"I'll have to go for the constable," he said. "You'll be safe in your room. Change from those wet things. I don't want you to be ill."

He sounded so gentle, so solicitous, I nodded. "I'll have the constable see that Newgate is picked up as well. Go upstairs now." He released me reluctantly and I climbed the steps. He waited until I reached the top before he hurried out.

I lit the fire in the hearth and stripped off my sodden clothes, tossing them aside in a heap, then toweling myself briskly until my skin glowed warmly. I covered my gown with my heaviest robe and drew bedsocks on my feet before donning slippers. I fanned my hair by the fire to dry it, then brushed it back without bothering to tie it. When at last I heard horses and a carriage on the drive, I ventured downstairs again. There was no light under Juliette's door. I prayed fervently that she would sleep through the excitement. It would be trying enough for her to face the news of Charles' death in the morning.

Paul bounded through the front door just as I reached the bottom of the steps. He looked so relieved, I had to smile. Through the open door, I saw the constable's men with lanterns setting out toward the woods in search of Lionel. The constable was leading Emma Mundy out to a carriage.

Paul took me in his arms. "It's over. Everything will be all right now. You must get some rest. I'll stay and wait for the others to come back."

"I could never sleep."

"There's nothing you can do tonight," he

said gently but firmly. "Juliette will need you tomorrow. It will be a difficult day." He put his arm about my waist and steered me firmly up the stairs. At the door of my room, he did not hesitate but guided me directly to the bed and lifted my feet as though I were a helpless child. But I did not resent it. I was so glad of his presence and his strength. I had only known him a few days, yet my heart sang at his every touch. I smiled as he drew the quilt over me and sat beside me, holding my hand. His strong fingers were warm against mine.

"I'll stay the night. You and Juliette shouldn't be alone," he said firmly. "We'll talk in the morning." He bent and pressed his lips gently to mine. "Sleep now, darling." He extinguished the lamp and left me alone.

I lay a long time with the memory of his kiss warming me. All my fears had vanished. Even the painful knowledge that Charles was dead did not completely dispel my relief and happiness that the dreadful mystery of Harrowgate had come to an end. Despite my certainty that sleep would elude me, I was exhausted and soon fell into deep slumber. I dreamed of great balls in the east wing, of Elizabeth Ashcroft Beaumont with her glittering diamonds, but there were no ghostly apparitions to disturb my rest. Like me, they were at peace.

When I finally opened my eyes, the room was light and it took me several moments to recall the eventful night that had passed. I washed and dressed hurriedly and went downstairs. Paul was in the dining room, where the table was laid for two. He touched my hand as he drew my chair and seated me.

Becky Riker came in smiling and carrying a tray of steaming eggs and a covered toast rack. Her faced sobered when she saw me.

"Oh, when I heard what happened because of my note—" The girl shook her head. "I meant no harm, only poor Annie—"

I patted her arm. "I know that, Becky. Is Juliette all right?"

She nodded. "Still sleeping. I'll fix her a tray in a bit."

"And Annie? Did they send someone to her last night?"

Becky nodded solemnly. "M'mum went. The old woman's slipped into a coma again. Doctor says the end is near. She's vera old."

It was as though she had to finish one last thing before giving up the thin thread of life, I thought. She could not rest until she'd told me about Charles . . . and warned me about Jonathon—even though she hadn't been able to bring herself to betray him by name. For the worthless scoundrel he was, he had been good to her when she needed him.

When Becky left the room, Paul said, "Jonathon confessed everything. Seems he has a record in London and the police there have been looking for him for some time. He was using Annie's cottage to hide out."

"But he is related to her?"

"Her grandson. Anthony Newgate, Annie's son, was sent away as a young man—"

"Yes, I know part of the story."

He nodded. "Led rather an unsavory life in London, a common thief for the most part, gambling, drinking. Whenever he was hard up for it, he'd sneak back to visit his mother and she'd give him what she could but she wouldn't let him stay. She knew he was no good, but she couldn't stop loving him. According to Jonathon's story, Anthony swore he'd been cheated out of money owed him by young Beaumont, gambling debts—and that he'd been accused of stealing jewels Harland Beaumont had given him then taken back. He figured the Ashcrofts owed him and his family a lot more than the pittance promised to Annie when she retired."

"Harland Beaumont owed Anthony Newgate money?"

Paul shrugged. "It's possible, I suppose. A lot of young gentlemen were lured into card games by gamblers and then pressed for payment. Some months ago Jonathon ran into Charles in a pub in South Africa. Jonathon babbled his story, not realizing who Charles was, of course. Charles seemed very excited at hearing the diamonds had never left Harrowgate. He made the mistake of telling Jonathon who he was. There was a fight—the one Reggie and I broke up. Evidently, Jonathon followed Charles here. He moved into Annie's cottage so he could keep an eye

196

on Charles and find the diamonds."

My mind filled with memories from last night. Jonathon had said he would force me to show him where Charles had hidden the diamonds! That meant the diamonds *were* here at Harrowgate and that Charles had figured out where they were hidden! Was it possible that Anthony Newgate's story was true—that he had never gotten away with the diamonds at all? I closed my eyes and leaned back, trying to recall the ghostly scene I'd witnessed in the east wing. Anthony had run out with the diamonds—but Harland had gone after him. Had he caught him? Recovered his wife's gems?

"What is it, Margaret—?" Paul came around the table and touched my shoulder.

I looked up at him. "Jonathon insists the Ashcroft diamonds are here—he's the one who's been tearing apart the east wing searching for them."

"Well, he hasn't found them or he would have been long gone. I'm afraid the legend of the diamonds may be just that—a legend. Your great grandfather may have found them and chosen not to mention it. Anthony may have fenced them in London and lied to cover his tracks. There's no way of telling now."

"No, I think Charles figured out where they are. That was why he was going to be welcomed with open arms at Harrowgate and how he was going to be able to restore it to the splendid house it once was."

Paul frowned. "You could be right . . . and if he said a bit too much to the wrong people or in the wrong places—" He looked disturbed. "Neither of us knew very much about Reggie. If Reggie was on to the diamonds, he might have followed Charles here in hopes of cashing in on them. Jonathon wanted no competition, and he killed Reggie and Simpson." Paul looked at me most tenderly and drew me to my feet and into his arms. "He followed Charles to London when he left. He killed him. He confessed it last night."

"Oh—!" He let me bury my face in his shoulder and weep until some of the pain was gone. Then he raised my chin and dabbed at my eyes with his handkerchief. "He tried to make Charles tell him where the diamonds were hidden. They fought, and Charles was knocked unconscious and into the river."

I bit my lip.

"Try not to think about it now, darling." That was the second time he had called me by that endearment, and I felt safe and happy in his arms. I took his handkerchief and brushed my cheeks and dried my eyes. "I must go up to Juliette . . ."

"I'll tell Becky to wait with the tray."

"Yes . . ."

I walked up the steps slowly, dreading breaking the news to Juliette, yet knowing I was the only one who could do it. I found her sitting in bed, staring out at the gray sky and the mist on the windowpane. She turned without smiling.

I sat on the edge of the bed and lifted her hand into mine. Before I could speak, she said, "Charles is dead."

"How—?"

Her eyes were incredibly sad. "I dreamed it, only it was so real I knew it wasn't a dream. It was as if old Annie were telling me one of her visions. She used to do it often, you know, whenever your grandfather wasn't about. She was telling me that Charles was gone and that my tears would mingle with her own for our losses."

I stroked her hand. "We've both lost a great deal," I said softly. "You'll stay with me, of course . . ."

She withdrew her hand from mine and reached to the bedside table to pick up the snow dome Charles had given her. Slowly she turned it upside-down and held it on her palm while the flakes drifted down over the miniature village.

I watched as though hypnotized. How Charles and I used to laugh at the fascinating scene inside the tiny glass dome. How proud he was of his prize—and how carefully he always guarded it as one of his treasures in—

The tiger's den!

I jumped to my feet, telling Juliette I would be back. In the hall, I called to Paul who bounded up the stairs with a worried look on his face.

"What—"

"I know! I know where the diamonds are!"

He stared at me, and I pulled his hand forcing him to follow me. Becky had come up the steps with the tray and was gaping. "Take Juliette her breakfast and stay with her until I get back," I told her. Then I fairly raced along the hall to the door of the east wing. The door was still unlocked and I flung it open, not caring now about scurrying rodents or deep shadows.

"Where are we going?"

"To the ballroom. Oh, hurry, I know I'm right. If Charles hid anything, it would be in the tiger's den."

"What in the world are you talking about?"

"I remember now—Annie told me last night that Charles had left something for me there!"

We were in the upper hall, then descending the stairs rapidly. The doors to the ballroom were open as I had left them. I went immediately to the musicians' alcove and knelt in the dust at the side of the small raised dias. I began to tug at the last panel.

"Here, let me help you," Paul said. I moved aside and a moment later he had the panel off.

"You have to crawl in flat," I said.

He wriggled through the opening, coughing once or twice at the dust he stirred.

"To the left—"

How well I recalled Charles' little hole—a formation of floor supports that made a small crevice at the side of the crawl space under the stage. He called it his safe place where no

200

one would ever find the things he hid.

A few moments later, Paul scurried backwards like a crab out of the opening. He was covered with dust, his dark suit gray and his face streaked. But he was smiling as he held aloft a small brass bound cask and a flat package wrapped in cloth.

He laid them on the stage and stood to brush himself off. I stared at the objects, knowing they held the solution to the mysteries of Harrowgate. There was a small folded paper slipped under the clasp of the cask, and I pulled it out and opened it and swallowed the lump in my throat as I recognized Charles' writing.

"Dear Margaret—A chance meeting with a gent in a pub made me realize these baubles were still here at Harrowgate—and I was right. We'll live in style! Grandfather suspects I've located them, but since I have to leave so soon, best no one know where they are—only you and me. Remember how we always thought Annie meant *us* when she talked about the silly children in twin tigers' den? Guess Elizabeth Ashcroft knew the spot too and confided in her husband. The jewels were here all the time—only they were on the other side of the stage! Hang onto these if you find them before I get back. Love, Charles."

I handed the paper silently to Paul then unwrapped the packet that had been with the cask. It was the letter Annie and Dr. Foxx had spoken of. Only it wasn't a letter—it was Grandfather Franklin's will! I unfolded the thick parchment and read the words quickly. I could not stop the tears that overflowed my eyes. Harrowgate went to Charles, or to me at his death. Annie had her life-long pension in the cottage, and other servants were well remembered. A wavering codicil in the old man's spidery hand said he no longer trusted Wiley Temple or the Mundys, and he was giving the will to Annie to hide for safekeeping.

And Annie had worried about her grandson, so she'd hidden the will where only Charles and myself might think to look.

Silently, I handed the will to Paul and leaned over the small cask. I knew what it held, but I was unprepared for the glitter of the gems as I lifted the lid. Nestled in a soft bed of black velvet were the Ashcroft jewels. Even in the uncertain light of the ballroom, the diamonds winked and shimmered as I lifted the pendant and the ring that glittered like a queen's ransom.

The jewels that had brought so much unhappiness to so many people seemed suddenly released from their strange curse. From now on they would bring happiness, I was sure.

I turned and smiled at Paul. Arm in arm, we walked slowly back toward the main house to tell Juliette the good news.

Softly, Paul said, "Will you stay at Harrowgate?"

I considered the question, though I knew the answer in my heart. I had laid to rest the ghosts of the past. "I cannot stay on alone," I said quietly. "If Juliette wants to return to London when she's strong enough . . ." I would accompany her, and remain with her long enough to assure myself she was well taken care of and lacked for nothing.

"And if she wants to stay?" he asked, looking at me with his endearing blue gaze.

"So she shall. She will always have a home here."

He paused and turned so he faced me. His eyes were bright. "And what of me? Shall I continue to rent the Rutherford cottage and love you from afar?"

My pulse raced. Love. . . . I knew then that I loved him as well. His smile teased me. "Do you want to stay?" I whispered.

"More than anything I've ever wanted before."

I was in his arms then, returning his kiss with an ardor that I had never known myself capable of.

"Yes, I want to stay," he murmured against my lips.

I knew I had found complete happiness as we kissed again.

BESTSELLERS FOR TODAY'S WOMAN

THE VOW   (653, $2.50)
by Maria B. Fogelin
On the verge of marriage, a young woman is tragically blinded
and mangled in a car accident. Struggling against tremendous
odds to survive, she finds the courage to live, but will she ever
find the courage to love?

FRIENDS   (645, $2.25)
by Elieba Levine
Edith and Sarah had been friends for thirty years, sharing all their
secrets and fantasies. No one ever thought that a bond as close as
theirs could be broken . . . but now underneath the friendship
and love is jealousy, anger, and hate.

CHARGE NURSE   (663, $2.50)
by Patricia Rae
Kay Strom was Charge Nurse-in-the-Intensive Care Unit and was
trained to deal with the incredible pressures of life-and-death
situations. But the one thing she couldn't handle was her pas-
sionate emotions . . . when she found herself falling in love with
two different men!

RHINELANDER PAVILLION   (572, $2.50)
by Barbara Harrison
Rhinelander Pavillion was a big city hospital pulsating with the
constant struggles of life and death. Its dedicated staff of over-
worked professionals were caught up in the unsteady charts of
their own passions and desires—yet they all needed medicine to
survive.

SENSATIONAL SAGAS

FICTION FOR TODAY'S WOMAN

EMBRACES (666, $2.50)
by Sharon Wagner
Dr. Shelby Cole was an expert in the field of medicine and a novice at love. She wasn't willing to give up her career to get married—until she grew to want and need the child she was carrying.

MIRRORS (690, $2.75)
by Barbara Krasnoff
The compelling story of a woman seeking changes in life and love, and of her desperate struggle to give those changes impact—in the midst of tragedy.

THE LAST CARESS (722, $2.50)
by Dianna Booher
Since the tragic news that her teenaged daughter might die, Erin's husband had become distant, isolated. Was this simply his way of handling his grief, or was there more to it? If she was losing her child, would she lose her husband as well?

VISIONS (695, $2.95)
by Martin A. Grove
Caught up in the prime time world of power and lust, Jason and Gillian fought desperately for the top position at Parliament Television. Jason fought to keep it—Gillian, to take it away!

LONGINGS (706, $2.50)
by Sylvia W. Greene
Andrea was adored by her husband throughout their seven years of childless marriage. Now that she was finally pregnant, a haze of suspicion shrouded what should have been the happiest time of their lives.

Available wherever paperbacks are sold, or order direct from the Publisher. Send cover price plus 50¢ per copy for mailing and handling to Zebra Books, 475 Park Avenue South, New York, N.Y. 10016. DO NOT SEND CASH.